2

Just
South
of
Home

Just South of Home

of

Home

KAREN STRONG

Simon & Schuster Books for Young Readers

NEW YORK • LONDON • TORONTO • SYDNEY • NEW DELHI

SIMON & SCHUSTER BOOKS FOR YOUNG READERS
An imprint of Simon & Schuster Children's Publishing Division
1230 Avenue of the Americas, New York, New York 10020
This book is a work of fiction. Any references to historical events, real people, or real places are used fictitiously. Other names, characters, places, and events are products of the author's imagination, and any resemblance to actual events or places or persons, living or dead, is entirely coincidental.
SIMON & SCHUSTER BOOKS FOR YOUNG READERS
is a trademark of Simon & Schuster, Inc.
For information about special discounts for bulk purchases, please contact
Simon & Schuster Special Sales at 1-866-506-1949 or
business@simonandschuster.com.
The Simon & Schuster Speakers Bureau can bring authors to your live event.
For more information or to book an event, contact the Simon & Schuster Speakers
Bureau at 1-866-248-3049 or visit our website at www.simonspeakers.com.
Also available in a Simon & Schuster Books for Young Readers hardcover edition
Cover design by Laurent Linn
Interior design by Hilary Zarycky
The text for this book was set in Arrus.
Manufactured in the United States of America
0520 OFF
First Simon & Schuster Books for Young Readers paperback edition June 2020
2 4 6 8 10 9 7 5 3 1
The Library of Congress has cataloged the hardcover edition as follows:
Names: Strong, Karen, author.
Title: Just south of home / Karen Strong.
Description: First edition. | New York : Simon & Schuster Books for Young Readers,
[2019] | Summary: Twelve-year-old Sarah, her Chicago cousin Janie,
brainy brother Ellis, and his best friend, Jasper, investigate a tragic event in their
small Southern town's history.
Identifiers: LCCN 2018030146 | ISBN 9781534419384 (hardcover : alk. paper) |
ISBN 9781534419391 (pbk) | ISBN 9781534419407 (ebook)
Subjects: | CYAC: Family life—Georgia—Fiction. | African Americans—Fiction. |
Ghosts—Fiction. | Supernatural—Fiction. | Georgia—Fiction.
Classification: LCC PZ7.1.S79642 Jus 2019 | DDC [Fic]—dc23
LC record available at https://lccn.loc.gov/2018030146

To my grandmother Elnora,
who blessed me with a country girlhood

CHAPTER ONE
Red Velvet Miracle

It wasn't a mirage but a miracle. Two thick slices of red velvet cake sat on the table in front of us.

Ellis fidgeted on the couch next to me and struggled to keep his hands in his lap. My little brother knew he shouldn't make any sudden moves. No grabbing the fork on the linen napkin. No stuffing his face with cake. Not yet. For all we knew, it could be a trap.

Our grandma—who we *addressed* as Mrs. Greene—only made red velvet cake on holidays or for the Heritage Festival. Today was just a regular Sunday. This meant our grandma had baked the cake for *us*, which didn't make any sense. Mrs. Greene said I acted too much like Mama, and Ellis was a mannish hellion. I never thought in a million years I would get my grandma's county-famous cake served on her good plates for no reason.

Ellis and I sat frozen in Mrs. Greene's parlor, afraid to even breathe. Her fancy clock above the fireplace chimed four times and broke the silence. Mrs. Greene still wore her church clothes: a pale blue dress cinched at the waist and a strand of pearls around her neck. She didn't look like a grandma, which I guess was her intention. She was tall and slim with skin as bright as a sunrise, and her glossy black hair framed her face, which she had set in her trademark frown.

"What you two afraid of? It's cake not a snake. You can eat it."

Ellis jumped to the edge of the couch and grabbed his fork to take his first bite. Mrs. Greene didn't have to tell him twice. I scooted closer to the table and reached for my fork but stopped when Aunt Gina came into the parlor.

"I can't get over how big you two are getting! Growing like little weeds," she squealed.

Even though Aunt Gina now lived in Chicago, she was born and raised in Warrenville, so her voice remained slow and sweet. Aunt Gina was like a fun county fair that came to town once a year. Mama called her a free spirit. Today she wore red slacks with a bright blue blouse and funky purple shoes. Her hair was a halo of bouncy brown curls.

Several gold bracelets jangled on her arms as she pinched my brother's cheeks. Ellis grinned at her and then shoved another forkful of cake into his mouth. Red velvet crumbs fell into his lap. My brother had no worries. As long as his belly was full, he was happy. It didn't matter if he was eating in the lion's den. I knew better. Something weird was going on, and I had questions.

This morning Mama had told us we needed to come over to say good-bye to Aunt Gina and my cousin Janie. They visited every summer but never stayed long. A few days at most. This year wasn't any different. During every visit, Janie would constantly talk about Chicago. Bragging about the tall buildings and the bright lights. She called me backward country, but I didn't care. Who wanted to live in a place with so much concrete and not a stitch of grass? Janie claimed Chicago had plenty of grass, but that didn't matter to me. With all those city lights, I knew it would never get truly dark. I felt sorry for Janie. Nothing was more beautiful than a night sky so full of stars, you never felt alone.

Mama came out of the hall bathroom and stepped into the parlor. Her hair had puffed out from the humidity. Last night after she had flat-ironed it, she let me brush it in long strokes. I loved how some of her brown strands turned red in the sun. I wished I had Mama's dark skin, but I inherited Daddy's light tone, which got Mrs. Greene's approval. Ellis had Mama's deep complexion, but at least I had her brown-red hair.

In the parlor, Mrs. Greene, Aunt Gina, and Mama exchanged long and meaningful glances. Secret grown folks language. I couldn't tell if it was good or bad news.

"What's going on?" I finally asked.

Mama sat on the couch next to me. "Your aunt is taking a trip out west."

"You're not going back to Chicago?" I asked.

"No, pumpkin!" Aunt Gina was giddy with excitement. "I'm headed to California to do some more commercials."

"The ones where you play the fake dentist?" Ellis asked through his jam-packed-with-cake mouth.

Aunt Gina had filmed several commercials for Fresh Now! toothpaste. She played a dentist in a white coat who smiled too much and talked about tartar control and gingivitis. We even saw a couple of her commercials play down here on local TV. But Ellis was right—she wasn't a dentist. In the real world, she was a nurse.

"Yes, I'll be doing more of those but also some screen tests, too," Aunt Gina said.

"What's a screen test?" I asked.

"A bunch of mess," Mrs. Greene said. "Gina, you know nothing good is going to happen out there in Hollywood. You got too many stars in your eyes."

"I think it's great." Mama paused and touched my knee. "A screen test is like an audition for actors and actresses."

"You know California is where all the earthquakes happen," Ellis said.

Aunt Gina furrowed her brow. "That's true, but there haven't been any of those in a while."

"It only takes a big one to push everything into the ocean." Ellis wiped his mouth, leaving a trail of frosting across his cheek. "I once saw this movie where buildings crashed and people were out in the streets screaming—"

"Ellis," Mama interrupted. "Be quiet."

"Yes, ma'am." My brother went back to devouring his cake.

"Is Janie excited?" I asked.

Aunt Gina pulled a piece of imaginary lint from her pants, and her bracelets clinked together. She wouldn't look at me.

Mama cleared her throat. "Janie is going to stay here in Warrenville."

"Here at Mrs. Greene's house?" I asked.

"No," Mama said. "Janie will be staying with us."

"You know I still don't like this, Delilah," Mrs. Greene said. "These children need supervision. Especially Janie. Maybe if you stayed home instead of hemmed up at the Fairfield County courthouse, you could raise these children properly."

Mama took a deep breath. I knew she was counting to three in her head. Sometimes she did this before speaking to Mrs. Greene.

"Sarah is quite capable of taking care of things while I'm at work," she said.

This summer Mama had agreed to put me in charge and let me and Ellis stay at home by ourselves. I was tired of staying at Mrs. Greene's house. I would be turning thirteen at the end of September. I was mature and responsible. If my hair caught on fire or if Ellis broke a leg, I could get help from Mrs. Taylor, who lived next door. Our neighbor mostly stayed inside, watching game shows or her favorite house-wives on reality TV. Mama probably knew this, but she agreed to let us stay home anyway, and it had been an easy summer so far. Nothing bad had hap-pened, but that could all change if Janie stayed with us. Janie liked to get into trouble.

Mrs. Greene said an idle mind is the devil's work-shop, and Janie would have a lot of free time. It didn't help she loved using her five-finger discount to take what she wanted. Janie carried what she called a purse, but it was just a pink backpack full of her snoop prizes. Today at church I saw her stash away an MLK church fan. If Mrs. Greene found out that her citified granddaughter had stolen an image of Martin Luther King Jr. from the Lord's house, she would put a switch to Janie's legs.

"How long is Janie going to stay with us?" I asked.

"Just for two weeks," Mama said. "Until your aunt wraps up her commercials and screen tests."

Maybe I could make this work, and my summer wouldn't be totally ruined after all. Plenty of time to recover from this ordeal. All I had to do was keep my cousin out of trouble.

"Okay. It'll be fun, Mama," I lied.

Mrs. Greene sucked her teeth but remained silent.

Even she knew raising a child was a group activity in Warrenville. Grown folks took action first and asked questions later. Our town was small enough for word to travel fast about any trouble, but I knew there wouldn't be any. There hadn't been any kind of trouble in our town in a long time. I wasn't going to let Janie mess that up.

"Great!" Aunt Gina clapped her hands in celebration. "Janie is so looking forward to this."

"Where is she anyway?" Ellis finally finished his cake. His plate was spotless, as if he had licked it clean.

"Good question," Mrs. Greene said. "Sarah, go find that meddling girl. She's been too quiet."

CHAPTER TWO
Celebrity Daughter

I left the parlor and went upstairs to find Janie. I didn't come up here much because Mrs. Greene didn't like us rambling around without her.

When Ellis and I had spent our summers here, we were usually outside in the hot sun. Mrs. Greene believed the outdoors was where children belonged. She would slather us with sunscreen and make us wear hats. Heaven forbid we got a darker shade of brown. But playing in her yard and doing boring adult chores were totally different things. We did the latter. We planted marigolds and pulled up weeds. We made sure all the ferns on the front porch were properly watered. We spent most of our time digging in Mrs. Greene's garden so she could plant rows of cucumbers, melons, and squash. When she did let us inside the house, she left us on the screened back porch shelling peas or shucking corn. Other days I was on my hands and knees cleaning baseboards while Ellis wiped lemon oil on the wood furniture. And on the hottest summer days, when even she knew it was child abuse for us to be outside, we were at Mrs. Greene's beck and call, keeping her glass full of ice water.

This year I had finally escaped summer-work boot camp and now needed to make sure Janie's sticky fingers wouldn't put my freedom in jeopardy. I didn't want to be back in Mrs. Greene's clutches. Not even for a thousand red velvet cakes.

I peeked in Daddy's old room. Mrs. Greene had covered his bed in one of her patchwork quilts. Posters of Michael Jordan hung on the walls, and basketball trophies lined his dresser. The room was like a postcard from the past. I wondered why my grandma hadn't changed anything now that Daddy had his own house. Maybe she hoped he would leave Mama and come back home one day.

I looked into Aunt Gina's room, where Janie had been sleeping, but she wasn't there. Farther down the hallway, I stopped at Mrs. Greene's closed door. I turned the knob but found it locked as usual. My grandma always locked her bedroom and carried the key in her bra.

As I walked down the hall to check the bathroom, I noticed the attic door was ajar. I stood in front of it and hesitated. Was Janie up in the attic? Mrs. Greene wouldn't be happy if she found out.

I cautiously opened the door and looked up the dark stairs. The smell of mothballs and old furniture filled the air. Dust and cobwebs had settled into the cracks and crevices. A creepy feeling traveled up my spine. I hated dark places. When my eyes adjusted, I could see weak light coming from the attic windows.

"Janie, are you up there?" I whispered.

She didn't respond. I searched for a light, but I couldn't find one. Out of the corner of my eye, a shadow appeared at the top of the steps. I moved backward, and a shiver rippled through my body.

"Janie? Is that you?" I asked, a little louder this time.

The shadow didn't answer. My heart sped up. "You know you're not supposed to be up there." I didn't want to sound frightened, but I couldn't stop my voice from wavering.

The shadow whooshed down the attic stairs to meet me. Too fast for me to even run. Janie appeared in the dusky light, and I took a deep breath. I was mad at myself for being so scared. My cousin smirked.

"What were you doing up there?" I asked.

"Nothing." She had her pink backpack in her hands. The wooden handle of the MLK church fan poked out.

"Did you take something?"

"Nope." She zipped up her backpack. "I was just looking around. Mrs. Greene's got a lot of junk up there."

"I know you're lying. You were up there meddling." I winced as I used my grandma's words.

"Oh, so you're a lie detector now?" Janie brushed past me and went into Aunt Gina's room.

"Everybody is waiting for you downstairs."

She grabbed her suitcase from the end of the bed and began tossing in all of her stuff. Janie's box braids covered her face like a rope curtain, and her white halter top glowed against her bronze skin.

I scratched at the itchy cotton of my T-shirt. Mama wouldn't let me wear halter tops because my bra straps would show. She made me start wearing training bras this summer. Right before Memorial Day, we went to a fancy dress shop in Alton, where she forced me into a fitting room.

"How does it feel, honey?" Mama asked.

I frowned at her in the mirror.

"Don't pout, Sarah. Growing ladies need support. From this day forward, you're going to eat and sleep wearing a bra. You'll thank me later."

Janie had enough halter tops to fill each slot of the rainbow. I watched as she folded shorts, socks, and underwear. I didn't see any bras. Janie was flat chested, so she didn't have to go through my daily drama.

"Why don't you want to stay *here*?" I asked.

Janie swooped her braids over her shoulder. "Are you kidding me? Mrs. Greene is too crazy. And I'm sure not trying to be somebody's maid. No thank you."

"Are you happy about your mama going to California?"

"Of course." Janie collected her lotion and nail polish off the dresser. "This is just the beginning. It's only a matter of time before I become a celebrity daughter."

"Does this mean y'all are moving?" I asked. "What about all your stuff in Chicago?"

The thought of moving my things to another place made me cringe. I would have to pack up my books. All of them. Mama would then see how many I actually had and make me donate them to the Warrenville public library. How awful.

"Mom is taking care of all those details." Janie snapped her suitcase shut. "Why are you asking all these nosy questions anyway?"

"I'm just curious."

Daddy told me curiosity was an important trait of a scientist. Someday I was going to be an astrobiologist. I would find life on other planets, so I needed to have an inquiring mind. Questions were necessary. Janie just didn't want to give me any answers.

I picked up Janie's suitcase off the bed. "I can carry this downstairs for you."

Janie snatched it from me. "Don't touch my stuff."

"Don't be a spoiled brat," I shot back.

"Don't be a bossy nag." Janie turned away from me, and her braids smacked me in the face.

My cousin was only a year younger than me. Instead of acting her carbon age of eleven years, she could have passed for a toddler as she stormed out of the room.

I counted to three. Then to seven. It wasn't until I got to ten when the angry words melted on my tongue. Mama would have been so proud.

• • •

Everyone was waiting for us in the parlor. Daddy had just returned from putting gas in the SUV, because traveling to the Atlanta airport required a full tank. Janie was standing by the door with her face scrunched up like she'd smelled a rotten egg.

"I'm going to take the kids to the house." Mama kissed Daddy on the cheek. "I'll see you when you get back tonight."

Aunt Gina grabbed Janie into a tight hug. "You sure you don't want to ride with me and Uncle Robert to the airport? Send your mama off on her big California adventure?"

"Can't I just go with you?" she asked.

"It's only for two weeks. They'll go by so fast! Oh! I almost forgot. I got you a surprise." Aunt Gina pulled out a phone from her pocket.

Janie grabbed the phone and squealed. "This is for me?!"

"Now, don't get too excited with the call minutes," Aunt Gina said. "It's prepaid, so no calling up all of your friends in Chicago. This is only for you to call me. Whenever you want. Aunt Delilah can help you with the time difference."

Ellis moved from behind Mama and stared at Janie's new phone. "Can I get one of those?"

"No," Mama replied.

Aunt Gina hugged Janie again. "I'm going to miss you so much!"

Janie pulled away. "I could help you practice your lines, you know. It's not fair you're leaving me here in the boondocks. You know how much I hate it here."

"Warrenville isn't so bad," Aunt Gina said. "You'll get to know your cousins better and have so many new adventures."

"I doubt it." Janie crossed her arms and frowned.

"Okay, everyone!" Mama said a little too loud and bright. "Time for Aunt Gina to hit the road."

We all congregated on the porch. Aunt Gina hugged and kissed Mrs. Greene. Despite my grandma's misgivings, she pushed a huge plastic bin of red velvet cake slices into Aunt Gina's arms. When she got into Daddy's SUV, Aunt Gina waved wildly at Janie, but my cousin ignored her; instead she climbed into the backseat of Mama's car and stared out the window in the opposite direction.

While Mama put Janie's suitcase in the trunk, I got in the front passenger seat. When I turned around, Janie's brave face was crumbling. Little tears formed at the corners of her eyes, and her lips had started to quiver. So I acted how I would want someone to do for me if I was about to cry. I turned away and pretended like I hadn't seen anything at all.

Janie sniffled, but she didn't speak. By the time Ellis and Mama had gotten in the car, Janie's eyes were dry. Her brave mask restored.

"Okay, everyone ready to go?" Mama asked.

Ellis clicked his seat belt. "Let's escape while we still can!"

Janie jutted out her lower lip and remained silent.

Mama turned to me. "You ready?"

"Let's go home, Mama," I said confidently.

CHAPTER THREE

Planets and Moons

The drive from Mrs. Greene's house was quiet except for the huge burp from Ellis. I had given him my slice of red velvet cake, and, instead of taking it home for later, he had eaten it on the spot. I'm convinced my brother has a tapeworm.

I pulled down the visor and peeked at Janie in the mirror. She was staring out the window with the same rotten-egg look on her face. There wasn't much to see in Warrenville. Trees, pastures, cows, more trees, and maybe another car if you were lucky.

Mama drove up to the house and parked in the garage. Ellis and I got out of the car, but Janie didn't move a muscle. She continued to stare at the empty space in front of her.

"Why she looking so weird?" Ellis asked.

"Janie? Are you ready to come in?" Mama asked.

My cousin slowly stepped out and looked around. She stared at our bikes and Daddy's power tools. Hopefully she wasn't getting any ideas of putting our things in her backpack. She probably didn't even have that much room left.

Ellis started to take Janie's suitcase out of the trunk, but she quickly grabbed it from him. "Keep your hands off my stuff."

"I don't want your raggedy suitcase," he said.

"Ellis, be nice. Janie is our guest," Mama said.

"She's a hostile guest!" Ellis protested.

"Excuse me?" Mama's voice had a thread of warning. "What did I just say about being nice?"

"Yes, ma'am," he mumbled.

Janie smirked and followed Mama inside. She didn't see Ellis making monster faces behind her back.

Our house wasn't as spotless as Mrs. Greene's house. It wasn't dirty, but you could tell people lived here. Mama's law office papers were strewn across the kitchen table. Daddy's empty coffee cup was still on the counter. In the den, Ellis had his latest model car project on top of old newspapers. My books were stacked high on the couch. An artifact of each person who lived here, a clue to our favorite things.

Mama put her purse on the kitchen table. "Janie, you'll be staying up in Sarah's room. She's got plenty of space."

My best friend, Jovita, had twin beds, so I'd thought I should get twin beds too for our sleepovers. It was better than my old pink canopy bed, which looked too much like a baby crib. But lately I wasn't sure if I had a best friend anymore. Jovita and I hadn't spoken since Yvonne Jones's sixth-grade graduation party. Jovita had been invited. I had not. Everyone knew Yvonne hated me. Especially Jovita. So I was hurt when she went to the party without me. Right now she was in Stone Mountain, visiting her daddy for the entire month of June. Friendships were so confusing. I wished a best friend came with an instruction manual; then I would know exactly how to deal with Jovita. It would make everything so much easier.

Now having twin beds was a good thing. I didn't want to play footsie with my cousin at night.

"I'll take you up to my room," I said.

We walked through the den to the foyer. Janie stopped in front of the staircase and continued to look around, scoping. I would have to tell her this wouldn't be tolerated. If Mama found out Janie took something from us, she would think I couldn't handle the responsibility, and I would be Mrs. Greene's personal butler again.

Janie followed me up the stairs to my room. I took a deep breath before I opened the door. After sixth-grade graduation, I had decided to redecorate. Daddy helped me paint the walls a few weeks ago. I had picked a color called Liquid Blue because it reminded me of the ocean, and water meant life. At least that's how life started on our planet. Mama picked out the floral comforters for my twin beds. I put up posters showcasing everything I liked best. Most of them were the planets of our solar system, including Pluto. I also had a poster of Saturn's moons. Enceladus was my favorite moon because near its south pole, plumes of water shot into space and fell back down to the surface as snow.

I had left the wall above my guest twin bed empty. I had been waiting for Jovita to pick out some of her favorite things to decorate it, but she hadn't told me anything yet. Maybe her daddy didn't like her talking on the phone? Maybe she was waiting for me to send another e-mail? I tried not to think about the other reason she hadn't contacted me. It tied my stomach in knots. I wasn't the type of girl who giggled about boys and got invited to parties. I was a girl who lived inside her head and read books about planets. I should have known a meteor event like getting invited to Yvonne's party would make our friendship extinct.

"You can put your stuff on that side of the room," I said.

"Okay, whatever." Janie dropped her suitcase and backpack on the bed. "Who's that woman?" she pointed to a poster hanging above my desk.

"That's Mae Jemison," I said. "She was the first black woman to travel in space."

Janie rolled her eyes. I watched as she sat next to her suitcase and judged my room. She frowned at my posters. She sneered at my astronomy books. She shook her head sadly at my spaceship clock. Instead of upsetting me, I was happy none of my stuff sparked her interest. I didn't have to worry about anything slipping into her pink backpack when she left.

Janie pulled out her nail polish. "I'm almost out of my favorite shade, but I'm so deep in the country I can't even get to a mall for a new bottle."

"We have a mall," I protested. "Not in Warrenville, but we can drive to Alton. Mama can take us on Saturday if you want."

Janie ignored me and took out another bottle of nail polish.

I wasn't entirely sure how I was going to keep this city girl entertained. We only had Town Square in the center of Warrenville and not much to see. Marigold Park featured a few benches and tables with a swing set and a basketball court. Loren's Grocery was about as big as our two-car garage. We had a post office and a public library that was only open three days a week. Hawkins Hardware, Lucille's Consignment Shop, and Dunbar's Ice Cream Parlor were the other main attractions. Everything else was in Alton, a university town about twenty miles away.

The only interesting place in Town Square was the Train Depot, but I wasn't sure if I could take Janie there. Mrs. Whitney was the owner and had recently moved back to Warrenville after being away for a long time.

Daddy told me that Mrs. Greene and Mrs. Whitney used to be friends once, but it was so long ago that no one remembered. My grandma now claimed Mrs. Whitney was a root witch. I didn't dare ask Mrs. Greene any more about it because she would say I was minding grown folks business.

I first met Mrs. Whitney at the post office when

she told me every little detail about her deceased husbands. Mrs. Whitney had been widowed four times. She was now engaged to Sylvester Coolidge, my granddaddy's business partner, which probably wasn't good news for him, knowing all her other husbands were dead.

"Sam was the nicest," Mrs. Whitney had told me, "Rufus was the most handsome. Dooley was a true gentleman, but Lionel was the richest. I miss him the most. God bless his money."

She'd used Lionel Whitney's money to buy and remodel the Train Depot. She opened it up for business earlier this summer, where she ran a history center and a gift shop.

Maybe Janie wouldn't mind staying in the house, watching TV, and going to church with us on Sundays. But I knew deep down Janie wouldn't be satisfied. It was in her nature to want to explore and get into trouble. And I would have to make sure that didn't happen, a two-week challenge since Janie and I didn't have anything in common.

It was going to be a long two weeks.

CHAPTER FOUR

Ghost Story

Janie unpacked her clothes and put them in the top two drawers of my dresser. She didn't take anything else out of her backpack. I was curious to know if the MLK church fan was her only snoop prize. So far I had just seen her nail polish collection. Jovita liked bold colors, the ones I was too shy to try. I stared at the bright yellow polish on Janie's toes. I couldn't remember the last time I had a pedicure. I wore sneakers, even though Mama said that I should let my feet breathe every once in a while.

Ellis appeared in the doorway. I frowned because he had Walter on his shoulder. Janie wasn't paying attention. When he sat next to her on the bed, it only took her two seconds to yelp.

My brother petted his bearded dragon. "Don't be scared. Walter won't bite you unless he thinks you have a cricket in your hand."

Walter blinked and darted out his tongue. "Get that thing away from me!" Janie screamed as she sprang from the bed.

"Ellis, you shouldn't have Walter in here," I said.

"Walter is a part of our family."

"Not everyone likes lizards. You know what Mama said about pushing Walter on people. Put him back in his terrarium."

Ellis pouted but got up and left.

Janie scrunched up her face. "Nasty."

"It could have been worse," I added. "He wanted a tarantula, but Mama told him no."

As night settled in, Janie lay on her bed and read a celebrity gossip magazine. Aunt Gina had brought a whole stack of them from Chicago. Glossy covers with headlines of movie stars battling heartbreak and backstabbers. Janie read them, mesmerized, preparing for her next life as a celebrity daughter.

I sat at my desk and wondered if I should go downstairs to Mama's office and check my e-mail. Maybe Jovita had finally replied to my message. She would be back in town for the Heritage Festival in mid-July, which was the same weekend as her birth-day. We usually planned her party together, but since we hadn't talked, I had no idea what she was going to do. Bubbles filtered up in my stomach, and I tried to swallow my doubts.

Ellis eventually came back into my bedroom. He had changed into his nightclothes and smelled of mint toothpaste.

"What do you want now?" I asked him.

"I'm trying to be nice to our guest."

Janie yawned and turned a page in her maga-zine. "You're not doing such a good job. Where's the chocolate on my pillow? Where's my fluffy bathrobe? Where's my room service?"

"This ain't no hotel," Ellis replied.

"I'm bored," Janie said. "Entertain me."

Ellis sat on my bed with his signature grin. I knew where this was going. "You wanna hear a ghost story?"

My brother's best friend, Jasper Johnson, was a big influence on him. Jasper was the big brother Ellis had always wanted. I didn't take it personally. Jasper was twelve like me, and at one time I thought we could trade thoughts about astronomy. I always sparked his interest when I talked about radio tele-scopes and aliens but then quickly lost it when I went into the mineral composition of planets. So when he came to the house, I usually left him alone to play video games with Ellis.

Jasper had recently become obsessed with ghosts, ever since he started working for Mrs. Whitney. She had told him one of the reasons she came back to Warrenville was to rid the town of restless spirits. Of course he shared this with Ellis. Nowadays, it was only a matter of time before my little brother would bring up Creek Church.

"Don't go spreading lies," I said.

"Janie, do you want to hear a Warrenville ghost story?"

Janie dropped her magazine. Ellis had gotten her attention. "Yes."

Ellis rubbed his hands together and grinned. "Creek Church is this old place out in the woods."

"None of this is true," I added.

"Let him tell the ghost story," Janie said. "Unless you're scared of having nightmares."

"You know better, Ellis," I said. "You're just going to scare yourself. You already sleep with two night-lights."

"I ain't afraid of the dark!"

Ellis was ten and the baby of the family, so he

tried hard to be brave, but I wasn't going to partici-
pate in my brother's shenanigans. He didn't need the
ghost story to be true; he just needed it to be spooky.
If anyone was going to have nightmares, then it
would be him.

"You know the place where we went to church
today? That's not the original location. They had to
move it because the old church was haunted."

"They moved to a new church because the Klan
burned the old church down," I corrected him.

Missionary Creek Baptist Church was on the
east side of Warrenville, not far from Mrs. Greene's
house. We attended most Sundays, and sometimes
Mama dropped us off alone if she was working hard
on a case. At least she didn't make us go to Sunday
school anymore. The teachers complained because I
asked too many questions. The original location—the
one Ellis was hawking as haunted—was on the other
side of town.

"Oh, Creek Church is haunted," Ellis said. "When
they tried to rebuild the old church, strange things
would happen. One time, it rained dead birds. They
fell straight out of the sky. And the bricks they laid
turned to dust. Another time, blood seeped up from
the ground. Flooding everywhere! After that, the

police kept getting calls of weird lights coming from the woods at night. In the end, grown folks said haints wanted the place for themselves, so they left it alone."

"What are haints?" Janie asked.

"Restless ghosts," he said.

Grown folks in Warrenville loved stories about haints. I didn't believe any of them. I knew it was just a way to keep kids in the house at night. The only streetlights were in Town Square so when night fell, it was pitch black.

"Where's this place?" Janie asked.

"At the end of Linnard Run," Ellis said. "Not too far from my friend Jasper's house. He's the one who told me all about Creek Church."

"It's an old forgotten dirt road," I said.

"These haint things live at this Creek Church place?" Janie asked. "Have you been there?"

Ellis's eyes opened wide in shock. "I ain't about that life. I don't want to get the curse."

"Curse? What curse?" Janie asked.

"Mrs. Whitney warned Jasper never to take anything from Creek Church. Doesn't matter what it is. A leaf off a tree, a pinecone, a rock. Doesn't matter. A haint will follow you to your house and cause trouble until you bring back what you took."

"How do you know that's true?" she asked.

"It's not true Janie," I said. "Ghosts don't exist."

Mama came into my bedroom wearing her floral silk robe. She had taken off her makeup and put her hair up in a top knot.

"It's getting late," she said. "You should all get to bed. Especially you, Ellis. It's way past your bedtime."

Ellis hugged Mama tight, and she kissed him on the top of his head before he left for his bedroom.

Mama sat on Janie's bed and touched her braids. "You're good and settled?"

"Yes, Aunt Delilah," Janie said.

Mama looked at me. "Any plans tomorrow?"

I automatically went to my usual plans of keeping Ellis entertained with his model car projects and reading my books, learning more about Saturn's moons. That wasn't going to fly with Janie here.

"What if I take Janie to Town Square?"

Mama tilted her head and thought for a moment. "Make sure you let Mrs. Taylor know when you leave."

"Aunt Delilah, do you think I could call my mom now?" Janie asked.

"Not yet, honey. She's still in the air, and when

she lands in California, it'll be too late here. Let's try tomorrow, okay?"

Janie's face cracked in disappointment.

When Mama left, Janie slid her backpack under the bed. She got out a nightgown from her suitcase, and I took out my pajamas. Awkward silence filled the space between us.

"There's an ice cream parlor in Town Square. What's your favorite kind?" I asked her.

She ignored me and grabbed her toothbrush. Just before leaving my room, she turned to face me. "I hate ice cream," Janie said. "Just like this place."

CHAPTER FIVE
Good Hostess

The next morning the smell of Daddy's coffee and the sound of Mama's voice filtered up to my room. I usually got up easily, but this morning my eyes stuck closed, and my body wouldn't let go of sleep. Getting Janie settled had sapped all of my energy. When I finally pulled my legs out of my warm bed and walked downstairs, my parents had finished breakfast.

"We missed your company this morning," Mama said.

Daddy sat at the kitchen table drinking his coffee. I usually sipped alongside him, although he liked his coffee black, and I filled my mug with sugar and cream. As a little girl, I had believed he was an undercover superhero like Clark Kent, there to save me from anything. Now that I was older, I learned there were some things Daddy couldn't do. He couldn't rescue me from the faint panic floating in my chest about my friendship with Jovita. He couldn't make her call or e-mail me. He couldn't prevent Janie from causing trouble and putting snoop prizes in her pink backpack.

I sat at the kitchen table, and Mama kissed the top of my hair puff. "I know you'll be a good hostess for Janie during her stay."

Daddy drained the rest of his coffee. "You're taking Janie to Town Square today?"

"Yes," I said. "I was also thinking we could stop at the Train Depot and visit Mrs. Whitney."

My parents exchanged looks. Daddy got up to rinse out his coffee mug. "Don't let Mrs. Whitney start filling your head with any of her tall tales. Your grandma wouldn't approve."

"That woman never approves of anything," Mama said.

Daddy chuckled. "That may be true, but you know how she feels about Mrs. Whitney."

"Why don't they like each other?" I asked them.

"Well, currently she wants to have a séance in

Marigold Park," Daddy said. "The festival board wasn't happy."

"What's a séance?" I asked.

Mama gave Daddy a weary look and placed her hands on my shoulders. "Mrs. Whitney just wants to help the community find closure with their loved ones who have passed on. She's eccentric, but she means well."

"The festival board disagrees," Daddy said. "They denied her booth. That woman is causing more trouble than it's worth."

The Heritage Festival was an annual summer event, always held on the third Saturday in July to celebrate our community of Warrenville. Mrs. Greene already volunteered me to help out with her booth. It was also the time of year where the townsfolk of Warrenville, Alton, and all of Fairfield County had access to a slice of her famous red velvet cake. Mrs. Greene would take the money and make a donation to help the sick and shut-in. My grandma was also on the festival board. I'm sure she had voted against Mrs. Whitney's booth.

"Mrs. Whitney has gathered a wealth of knowledge about the history of this town. I believe you ladies could learn a lot from her by visiting," Mama said.

I smiled. In that moment, I received the stamp of approval to go inside the Train Depot.

"Just remember, Sarah," Daddy said. "No tall tales."

The house remained quiet while Janie and Ellis slept. In the bathroom, I brushed out my hair, and it billowed away from my head like brown-red cotton candy. I parted my hair down the middle with the stick handle of my comb, and rubbed mango butter between my fingertips, then proceeded to braid it. Being left-handed, it took me longer to learn, but now I could plait and cornrow with the best of them. After I finished, I smoothed two long French braids around the curve of my neck and secured them with hair ties.

When I walked into my bedroom, Janie was still burrowed underneath the covers. I quickly put on my training bra and pulled on my Andromeda T-shirt. This was the galaxy that was going to collide with our Milky Way. It would happen four billion years in the future, but sometimes that fact kept me up at night. After tugging on some shorts, I grabbed my flip-flops instead of my sneakers. Mama was right about my feet needing to breathe in this heat.

I went downstairs and resumed watching the *History of the Solar System* series. For my birthday in September, Daddy was taking me to the science symposium in Atlanta and I couldn't wait to go. I had already prepared several questions about natural variation and artificial selection. I was sad my plans for snuggling on the couch and studying the episodes were squashed with Janie's prolonged stay.

During the opening credits of the second episode, I heard Ellis trudging down the stairs. He came into the den and blocked my view of the TV.

"Get out of the way," I said.

"I want to fry an egg."

"You need to eat the cereal I left out for you."

"I want a hot fried egg," he whined.

"Don't be a baby, Ellis. Mama said you can't cook anything."

"You can watch me. Isn't that your job? To watch me?"

"Eat the cereal," I said. "Or you can eat air. Your choice."

Janie came down next, rubbing her eyes. She had on a red halter top and jean cutoff shorts. Her box braids hung around her shoulders.

"Why is everyone up so early?"

I looked at the clock on the wall. It was almost ten a.m. "It's kind of late, Janie."

She sat in Daddy's recliner and stared at the books stacked beside me on the couch. "Are you in summer school?"

In addition to checking out books from the Warrenville public library, Daddy had bought me a thick book about NASA's Cassini mission to Saturn. I was up to the moon Titan, which contained the right chemistry for life, even though the oceans were liquid methane.

"I'm working on a research project," I said. "I'm going to a science conference in September."

"Will you fry an egg for me?" Ellis asked Janie.

"I hate eggs," she replied.

After they ate, Janie went upstairs, and Ellis immediately started to work on his model car. My brother loved tearing things apart and then putting them back together. Daddy said it was a good sign of his engineering skills. Last year, when Ellis tore apart the toaster oven to see how it worked, Daddy decided to give him specific projects so he wouldn't move on to bigger things like the washing machine or the lawn mower. Lately, Ellis had been building model cars.

"When you get ready to paint that thing, you'll have to go outside," I said.

"I know."

"You're going to have to paint it on Mrs. Taylor's porch," I added.

"Why?"

"Janie and I are going to Town Square, and I can't leave you here by yourself."

"I don't wanna go to Mrs. Taylor's house," Ellis said. "It smells like cough syrup and musty feet."

"That's the deal," I said. "Unless you want to come with us."

"I'll stay here," Ellis grumbled.

I went upstairs to get some of my allowance money. As I neared my doorway, I heard Janie's voice. She was leaving a voice message for her mama.

"Mom, it's me. I called you late last night. I still wish you had let me come with you. I hate it so much here. Sarah is a loser nerd, and Ellis is a whiny baby. I can't wait until you come back and get me."

I leaned on the wall next to my doorway; anger crawled up my neck and made my face itchy and warm. I shouldn't have been surprised, but it still hurt a little to hear Janie saying those mean things about me. I tried to remember the promise I'd made to Mama. I was going to be a good hostess even if Janie was a hostile guest. I made a coughing noise

39

and shuffled my feet to let her know I was in the hall.

"Okay, I better go," Janie said. "Please call me back."

When I walked into the bedroom, Janie was sitting on the bed, shoulders slumped, her long braids hiding her face. She looked sad and lonely.

"You still want to go to Town Square?" I asked.

"Whatever." She grabbed her backpack. "I'll wait for you downstairs."

When she walked out of the room, I got some money out of a hidden compartment in my jewelry box. I no longer felt bad for hiding the money. Janie couldn't be trusted. She didn't even like us.

I would have to deal with my cousin for two weeks: fourteen days of her complaining, 336 hours of her badmouthing my town, 20,160 minutes of her snooty I'm-better-than-everybody behavior. I could do this though. Earth was almost five billion years old. It could be worse.

There was one thing Janie and I had in common. I couldn't wait for Aunt Gina to come back to get her. Mrs. Greene said that you should love your blood kin, but you don't have to like them. Right now, I liked my training bra more than Janie.

CHAPTER SIX
Silver Hands

Janie and I walked out of my neighborhood to Main Street, then traveled across to the railroad tracks. The trains didn't come through Warrenville anymore. Nothing much came through our town. Everyone worked or went to school in Alton, which was the Fairfield County seat. Not too many kids lived in Warrenville either. Ellis called it Old People Central. Jovita complained about this endlessly. We were always the only two girls on the school bus for the ride to Alton. Maybe this was the real reason we became friends. Jovita hated our small town, but I couldn't imagine living anywhere else. Warrenville was somewhere I belonged. I liked the way everyone knew my name and my family. You always felt like you were home.

"After I show you around, I have some money to buy us ice cream," I said.

Janie tugged on her backpack straps and sighed. "I told you I hate ice cream."

I wasn't good at small talk. I usually stayed quiet and listened to Jovita talk about anything and everything. So right now, I didn't know what to say in response to Janie's negativity.

"What do you like, then?" I asked. "Nail polish? Magazines?"

"I can tell you what I don't like," Janie sneered. "Small country towns. Loser nerds who read space books."

The angry heat beneath my skin returned. Mama told me sometimes people say mean things because they're sad. That didn't mean it hurt any less.

We walked in silence as Janie followed me down the railroad tracks to the Train Depot. The building was painted bright yellow with a brown tin roof; it was built like a shotgun house. There were two entrances because during Jim Crow days there were two of everything. Now the Coloreds Only door was the entrance for the history center, and the Whites Only door was for the gift shop. A CLOSED sign hung in front of the window of the history center, so we went into the gift shop. A crystal chime tinkled above our heads, and both of us sighed in relief as soon as we felt the coolness of the air conditioner chugging away in a window. The wood floor gleamed in the sunlight. The shop was filled with all types of doodads. Canned jellies and chow-chow relish. Tall rotating towers of magnets and postcards clustered in front of a glass display counter.

Janie's face brightened with glee. My heart skipped a beat. My cousin with her pink backpack was in pickpocketing heaven. I would have to watch her sticky fingers closely and not let them out of my sight.

In the back of the gift shop, a door creaked open, and Mrs. Whitney walked toward us. Her silver hair fell in tight curls across her shoulders, and blue eye shadow glimmered on her dark brown skin. Three thick necklaces draped over her white dress. The longest necklace had a large black stone. When she saw us, she touched it.

"Sarah Greene. Welcome. I believe this is the first time I've seen you in my store."

"Yes, ma'am," I said.

"Is that Gina's child with you?" She studied Janie, who frowned at her.

"I have a name. It's Janie."

Mrs. Whitney smiled. "Same name as the character in my favorite book."

"What book is that?" Janie asked.

"*Their Eyes Were Watching God.* It's a bit too grown for you to read right now, but one day it may speak to you. Maybe that's who your mama named you after."

Janie cracked a small smile but quickly focused her attention back on a display of peach preserves.

"Janie is visiting for two weeks," I said. "I'm giving her a tour of Town Square."

"What a blessing," Mrs. Whitney replied. "Take a look around and let me know if you need any help."

I followed Janie down one of the aisles. Her fingers moved across the merchandise, but nothing had gone into her pockets or her backpack. At least not yet.

At the rear of the gift shop, strange red candles filled a shelf. Small statues of black Virgin Marys, their hands raised in praise were on another. There were small bags of cloth stuffed with fragrant herbs that filled my nose with sour scents. Janie reached out to touch them.

"Leave it alone," I said.

"It's just potpourri," she snapped.

"I don't think so."

Next to the fragrant bags were several stuffed dolls with misshapen arms and mismatched buttons for eyes. The dolls had small horseshoes and four-leaf clovers sewn on their chests. They were creepy. The cold twinge on the back of my neck told me that these dolls weren't made for playtime. These items didn't seem like a gift you would give to someone. Not unless you wanted to scare them. Or curse them.

A loud bump against the wall made both of us jump. After a muffled crash, the back door opened, and a tall boy with several boxes in his hands smiled at us.

"Sarah, what are you doing here?"

Jasper Johnson put down his boxes. He wore a dirty T-shirt and jeans. His ruddy brown skin was covered in sweat, but at least he had a fresh haircut, buzzed low with sharp geometric lines. His daddy was a barber and practiced a lot on Jasper's head.

Janie examined his clothes with disdain. "Who are you?"

"This is my brother's friend, Jasper," I said. "He's helping out Mrs. Whitney this summer."

"You must be Janie," Jasper said. "I've heard a lot about you."

My cousin crossed her arms and gave me a dirty look. "I bet you have."

"Why does Mrs. Whitney have all this creepy stuff in her store?" I asked.

Jasper picked up his boxes. "Customer demand. You would be surprised who comes in here and buys this stuff."

We followed him over to the other side of the aisle. In the corner, we stopped at a hanging display of silver hands. They dangled like teardrops, a blue eye in the center of each palm. A small army of trinkets.

"Take these, for instance." Jasper cocked his head toward the display. "These are one of our best sellers."

Janie reached up and touched one. They made a musical sound that reminded me of Aunt Gina's bracelets.

"These are pretty," Janie whispered.

"Protection from the evil eye," Mrs. Whitney said.

Janie jerked her hand away from the display. The shop owner had sneaked up on us.

"Evil is always around. Never sleeps," Mrs. Whitney continued. "It's our duty to be vigilant and to protect ourselves from it."

Janie tentatively reached back for a silver hand, rubbing her thumb over the blue eye. "Would this also protect you from haints?" Janie asked.

Jasper dropped his boxes with a muffled boom, and I bent down to help him.

"What do you know about haints, child?"

"She doesn't know anything about them," I said.

"Haints are restless ghosts. Right, Jasper?" Janie smiled at him.

Jasper's eyes widened. Daddy wouldn't like it if he found out that Janie and Mrs. Whitney had talked about haints. So much for no tall tales.

Mrs. Whitney touched the dark stone on her necklace again. "Haints are restless because they haven't yet found peace, but you leave them be. Don't mess with the spirit world, and it won't mess with you."

"It's time for us to go." I pulled Janie away from the spooky hands.

Mrs. Whitney followed us to the front of the store. "Girls, please do come back soon to visit the history center," she said. "I might have a thing or two that may interest you."

"Thanks, Mrs. Whitney." I pushed Janie toward the door.

We stumbled out of the Train Depot into the bright sun.

"Mrs. Greene is right," Janie said. "That lady is a root witch."

"She's not a witch," I said.

I took Janie to Lucille's Consignment Shop next. She wandered around the short aisles and complained about the old-lady clothes. I was thankful Lucille Hathaway wasn't at the shop today. She was in her early eighties, with a sharp tongue. No doubt Mrs. Hathaway would have schooled my cousin on her lack of home training. Instead, her great-grandson Toby was taking care of the shop. He was home from college, and he blinked at us with no comment.

At Loren's Grocery, Janie made a ruckus because they didn't carry any celebrity magazines. Sunnie Loren, one of the few high school girls who lived in Warrenville, popped her gum and nodded.

"Who you telling? They wouldn't know *Vogue* if it bit them on the toe," she said.

"How do you live here?" Janie asked. "I would go crazy."

"Biding my time," Sunnie said. "I'll be leaving soon."

They both got quiet when Mrs. Loren came

from the back of the store. "That's all this girl talks about. She can't wait to escape into the big wide world."

Sunnie widened her eyes in alarm; her mama had overheard the conversation.

"You don't need a fancy magazine, child. Read this newspaper and get informed. On the house!" Mrs. Loren gave Janie the *Alton Daily*. Janie grumbled but stashed it in her pink backpack.

I wanted to stop by the public library and pick up my requested books, but I didn't want to give Janie the satisfaction of calling me a loser nerd again. I would have to come back another time.

Our last stop was Dunbar's Ice Cream Parlor. After looking through the cold glass at the different barrels of flavors, I decided on strawberry, my eternal favorite. Despite saying she hated ice cream, Janie let me buy her a scoop of rocky road.

We sat in Marigold Park in the shade of the magnolia trees and ate our ice cream in silence. When I finished eating my cone, I stood up and stretched my legs.

"Ready to get back to the house?" I asked her.

"No," she said. "I want to go to Creek Church."

"We're not going there," I said quickly.

49

"Why not?" she asked. "You said it was just a burned-down place."

"It is. Which means there's nothing to see."

"So what's the big deal, then?" Her mouth twisted into a cruel smile. "Are you scared of the haints? I thought you didn't believe in any of that stuff?"

"I don't. It's just that . . ." I faltered.

Janie got up from the bench. "I think you're scared, and you don't want to admit it."

"There's no reason for me to be scared," I said.

Ellis never provided any proof that haints existed. Not even a sliver of concrete evidence. It would be silly for me to let a ghost story trick my nervous system into being afraid. The probability of that place being haunted was too low.

"Let's check it out," she said. "If you don't want to go, I'll go by myself."

"You don't even know where it is," I said.

"This town isn't that big. I'm sure I can find it."

I couldn't let Janie go anywhere alone. The last thing I needed was Janie wandering the back roads. What if she got lost? What if she fell and twisted her ankle? Worse, what if she got caught walking around by herself? The grown folks network of Warrenville would contact Mama in a heartbeat, and she would blame me. I would be right back at Mrs. Greene's house, raking up dirt.

"Fine. I'll take you," I said. "But it's going to be a total waste of time."

CHAPTER SEVEN

Creek Church

S top walking so slow," Janie called over her shoulder at me.

"You're the one walking too fast." I pressed my toes into my flip-flops and trotted behind her.

The afternoon sun was bright and hot above us. Sweat stuck to my T-shirt, and my bra straps itched. When we got to Linnard Run, we stood and stared. It was more like an old dirt path than a road. Between two rotten wood posts, a broken, rusty chain was on the ground. The NO TRESPASSING sign glared like a warning in the sunlight, but it was a weak barrier. I saw tire tracks in the dried mud, and several discarded soda bottles and beer cans littered the bushes. Somebody had been visiting this place.

Janie walked over the old chain and started down the narrow path. After a few moments I followed. Grass spilled out over the dusty edges and covered whole patches like carpet. The houses that remained had caved in with fallen tree branches and overgrown bushes. We walked in a forgotten place.

"Why is it so quiet?" Janie scratched her neck.

"Nobody lives here anymore," I said.

"Why?" she asked.

"I don't know. People left and moved to Alton. They went to bigger cities."

"I don't blame them," Janie said.

We finally reached the dead end; six stone steps were half-hidden behind tall weeds and wildflowers. They led up to a square stone slab slightly bigger than Mrs. Greene's parlor, shrouded in shade. It was all that remained of Creek Church. In the far corner, an old chimney barely stood, leaning toward collapse. Trash, burned bricks, and decaying wood lay scattered at its base. Behind the church ruins, the woods were thick and dark.

"This is it?" Janie frowned.

"I told you this would be a waste of time," I said. "You shouldn't believe everything Ellis says."

Janie held her arms tight by her sides and moved

through the thick weeds. She crept up the stone steps and pushed her sandals into the cracks.

"Come back!" I yelled.

Janie ignored me and continued up the steps. She walked across the stone slab to the chimney, then kneeled and picked something up.

"Get back here right now." I jumped at the sound of my loud voice. This place was too quiet.

She came back holding something in her hand. "Found a piano key."

"Put it back, Janie."

"It's broken anyway." She threw the ivory piece, and it clinked down the steps.

"Okay, you've seen Creek Church," I said from my spot in the road. "I brought you here. Now let's go."

She looked back at the woods. "I bet you there's a graveyard back there."

"Janie," I warned. "We need to get back to the house."

"Fine, don't come. Go hide in one of your books." Janie walked past the chimney and jumped down from the stone slab to venture farther into the woods.

I didn't want to follow her. But what if she fell into an old grave? There was another reason I didn't want to go into those woods. Maybe one I didn't want to admit. Something was off about this place. I hated that my brother's stupid haint story had gotten inside my head. I didn't believe in stuff like this. I believed in atoms and molecules. Not ghosts and curses.

I leaped through the dry weeds and walked up the steps. The slab was covered in old soot and dirt. A sudden wave of sadness rushed over me—being here and seeing the devastation caused. The Klan had burned down this church—racist men who hurt so many people for no reason other than the color of their skin. Daddy called them cowards who hid their faces behind white sheets and drove black cars in the dead of night. They were a part of Warrenville's dark history.

"Sarah!" Janie yelled.

I jumped from the stone slab to the ground and followed Janie's voice, heading deeper into the woods. My flip-flops seeped into the damp, mushy ground. The sound of Missionary Creek gurgled faintly in the distance.

I found Janie in front of a giant oak tree. All the other trees had green leaves, but the oak tree was bare and black. I stared at the gnarled branches reaching out like claws. A chill shimmied up my neck.

"Stay away from that tree." I pulled Janie away.

I continued to follow her as she wandered deeper into the woods, but I kept looking back at the black tree. The silence of the woods stuffed my ears like cotton.

Janie squealed. "See! I told you there would be a graveyard back here!"

"Stay out," I said.

Janie ignored me. I counted to three to keep from yelling at her and then kept going.

Tombstones covered with moss dotted the flat land, most of them broken or shattered to pieces. No one had taken care of them.

Janie paused and frowned at each tombstone. "I can't read any of these."

I stood close behind her. Six feet of dirt separated us from coffins and bones. I curled my toes in my flip-flops. Dead people made me jittery.

Janie walked to a far corner of the graveyard. After inspecting a spot behind the tombstone, she dug her hands beneath the top layer of dirt. I rushed over.

"Stop that! Are you crazy?"

"Check it out."

I looked into her dirty hand and saw a tiny locket. Only Janie would find jewelry in a graveyard. She rubbed the locket and blew off the remaining dust to reveal a face the color of bone: a woman in profile. She was bare shouldered and had her hair piled high on top of her head with curls cascading down her neck.

"It's a cameo," I said.

Janie slipped the locket into the front zipper of her backpack.

I widened my eyes in disbelief. "You can't take that."

"Who cares? Everybody here is dead."

"You shouldn't take things from here."

"What? You think that curse is real? You just told me that I shouldn't believe Ellis."

"You don't have the right to take things that don't belong to you," I said.

"I found it." Janie stood up and brushed the dried leaves off her knees.

"You never find anything." I pointed at her. "You take things."

A brisk breeze rippled through the leaves on the trees. It sounded almost like a whisper. "Did you hear that?" I asked.

Janie sighed and slung her backpack over her shoulder. "No, I didn't hear anything."

We walked out of the graveyard. I took care not to step on any of the old graves. The black oak was in our path. I held my breath as we neared the creepy tree.

As we passed it, the giant oak swayed and creaked. Out of the corner of my eye, I saw a shadow move in the tree. I shifted backward, afraid to turn away. My flip-flops hit my heels with sweaty slaps. When I reached the foundation of the church, Janie was already in the road, waiting for me.

"We don't have all day," she said.

I jumped up on the stone slab and turned to look at the black oak tree stark against the greenness surrounding it. Two shadows hovered above the branches. Stretching tall and thin, they floated to the ground. I turned and ran, rushing past the chimney and stumbling down the steps.

"What's wrong with you?"

"I think I saw something." I squinted my eyes to focus on the woods around us, but now I didn't see anything.

"Are you trying to scare me?" Janie asked. "You think that's funny?"

From out of nowhere, a boy jumped up on the stone slab. He was younger than us, maybe seven or eight years old. We both stared at him. He wore a torn cotton shirt and raggedy pants rolled up at the ankles. Red clay caked his bare brown feet.

"Is that who you saw in the woods?" Janie asked.

The boy walked toward us and stood at the top of the steps. He stared. The sunlight curved around him. A queasy feeling filled my stomach.

"Who are you?" Janie's voice was too high and too loud.

The boy didn't answer.

Ash marks covered his small brown arms, and his wooly hair was full of lint and dirt. Beads of sweat sprinkled across his forehead. In fact, he was drenched in sweat. My heart sped up. Something wasn't right.

Janie pressed her fingers into my arm. "Do you know him?"

"I've never seen him before."

Just as quickly as he appeared, the boy turned from us and walked away. When he passed the chimney, he turned back and smiled. Goose bumps blossomed up my arms. His smile held a secret. The boy jumped down from the slab and disappeared into the woods.

"We need to leave," I urged.

Janie must have been just as creeped out by the

boy, because she didn't argue and followed me a little too closely as we traveled as fast as we could back down Linnard Run.

I had never seen that little boy before. Maybe he lived in the Beaverdam Trailer Park and was exploring the woods. But then I thought about the shadows in the dead oak tree and I shivered. I tried to ignore the goose bumps lingering across my skin, but the standing hairs on my arms were a sure sign.

Creek Church was definitely more than just a burned-down place.

CHAPTER EIGHT

Stitches and Switches

Janie and I returned to the house and found Ellis on our porch painting his model car. When he saw us, he bolted up and started with the excuses.

"Mrs. Taylor told me I didn't have to stay at her house. The paint was too strong, and it was giving her a headache."

I didn't care that Ellis hadn't listened to me. My mind was still on the creepy shadows. I knew there had to be some kind of explanation. Maybe it was the sunlight coming through the leaves. I had read about illusions and how the brain could make you see things that weren't actually there.

Then that strange boy showed up. I hadn't come

up with a scientific explanation for him yet. He wasn't a shadow. He didn't look like a ghost. Maybe he was just a boy wandering the woods. Maybe he was lost. Those were the simplest explanations, even if deep in my heart I didn't believe them.

I wanted to forget everything I had seen at Creek Church and lose myself in my books. I didn't want to worry about things that I couldn't explain.

"I can see why Mrs. Taylor didn't want you on her porch." Janie fell into the porch swing and pushed off with her feet. "That paint stinks."

"Smells better than that perfume you sprayed all over the bathroom this morning."

"It's called Eternity Mist. All the movie stars wear it."

"You need to get a refund." Ellis rubbed his hands on his shorts, leaving blue paint streaks. "Y'all been in Town Square all day?"

I looked down at my watch and was shocked at the time. It was late afternoon. I didn't think we had been gone that long. Ellis could have burned the house down while I was away. I would have to be more careful. I rubbed my stomach. Although I only had breakfast and ice cream, I wasn't hungry. Creek Church had spooked my appetite.

"What did you eat for lunch?" I asked him. "You didn't cook anything, did you?"

Ellis sneered at me. "Lucky for you, Mrs. Taylor made me a fried bologna sandwich. Otherwise I would have starved waiting on y'all."

"Next time we go somewhere, you're coming with us," I said.

"Did you go to the Train Depot to see the root witch?" Ellis asked, using Mrs. Greene's words.

"She's not a witch," I replied.

"I don't know about that. She had some weird stuff in her store." Janie shrugged off her backpack and pulled out the cameo.

Ellis leaned in for a closer look. "What's that?"

"Duh, it's jewelry," Janie said.

I should have known Janie would want to flaunt that cameo. Now she would get Ellis all riled up.

"Why is it so dirty?" Ellis asked. "Where did you get it?"

"I found it in the graveyard at Creek Church."

"Are you crazy? Did you listen to anything I told you last night?!"

"I don't believe in your country curse," Janie replied.

"When I tell Mama, y'all gonna be in a heap of

trouble," he said. "You ain't even supposed to go to that place. It's off-limits."

"You're not going to tell Mama anything about this, Ellis," I said.

"Watch me," Ellis taunted.

"So you're a snitch now?" Janie jeered.

"I ain't no snitch!" Ellis yelled.

"You wouldn't last ten seconds in my neighborhood," Janie said. "Where I live, snitches get stitches."

"You gonna learn the hard way," Ellis said. "Things work different down here. Y'all got stitches, but we got switches."

"I'm gonna blame everything on you," Janie said. "You're the one who told me about that place."

"I was trying to warn you!"

They both stopped arguing when Mrs. Greene pulled up in our driveway. My heart lurched. The last thing we needed was our grandma finding out that we had been to Creek Church.

"This day just got worse," Ellis grumbled under his breath.

Even though we weren't staying at our grandma's house this summer, it didn't stop her from dropping by and checking up on us. She claimed it was for our well-being, but it seemed like she was secretly spying on us, trying to catch us doing dirty deeds.

"Don't you dare breathe a word," I warned Ellis.

Mrs. Greene closed the door to her sedan, smoothed out her white linen pants, and adjusted her matching long tunic. She stared at us as if searching for any sins we needed to confess. I broke eye contact with her and stared at my flip-flops, too scared she would see everything we had done today reflected in my retinas.

"Y'all look guilty about something," she said. "Sarah, come here."

I gave my cousin and brother a warning look and lumbered down the stairs to meet her. She crushed me into a strong hug, and I was enveloped in the flowery scent of her perfume. Mrs. Greene called it her signature fragrance. Mama called it mixing two cheap perfumes together. Maybe she needed a refund too.

"Why don't you be a good girl and hold my purse?"

Mrs. Greene shoved her white leather purse into my arms. I tried putting it on my shoulder, but it was too heavy.

"Your granddaddy used to hold my purse. Bless his soul," Mrs. Greene said. "It's good to see y'all outside in the fresh air. No need to be cooped up in the house."

She traveled up the steps and leered over at Mrs. Taylor's porch. The bickering reality-show house-wives she loved so much blared through our neighbor's screen door.

Mrs. Greene shook her head. "Not one drop of blood shared, yet your mama thinks Stella Taylor is qualified to take care of y'all. She treating you right?"

While our grandma insisted that we only call her by her proper name, she never quite gave other grown folks the same courtesy.

"Yes, ma'am," I said.

I guided Mrs. Greene straight into our living room. It wasn't as grand as our grandma's parlor, but it was the best room in the house.

She sat down in one of the plush chairs and sniffed the air while I stood with my hands together in a nervous grip. Ellis tried to sit down too, but I quickly stopped him. Mama would kill me if he got blue stains on her cream sofa.

"Doesn't smell clean in this house," Mrs. Greene said.

"It's paint." I faltered when she gave me a withering look. "Ellis is working on a project. Would you like some sweet tea?"

"Never needed it more," she said.

I rushed to the kitchen and poured sweet tea in a glass full of ice. When I came back into the living room, I caught Janie and Ellis in the middle of Mrs. Greene's inspections.

"You don't have any shorts with a respectable hem?" She tugged at the frays of Janie's cutoff jeans.

"When is the last time you got a haircut?" She narrowed her eyes at Ellis. "Looking like some kind of hoodlum. Doesn't make any sense."

When I gave Mrs. Greene her refreshment, she didn't stop drinking until it was all gone and then gave a small burp. "Who taught your mama how to make sweet tea? Not enough sugar. Tastes like leaf water. Are you sure her people are from Alabama?"

Mrs. Greene took a handkerchief from her purse and pressed it against her neck. The clocks in the living room filled the area with ticking noises.

Mama's family owned a clock business in Birmingham. Whenever Granddaddy Duncan sent her a new one, Mama would tear open the box with excitement.

"All this ticking is making me nervous." Mrs. Greene crossed her legs.

I sighed in relief when I heard the garage door

open. Mama was finally home from work. I met her in the kitchen.

"Mrs. Greene is here," I said.

Mama let out a heavy sigh. "Yes, I'm aware. I saw her car parked out front."

We went back to the living room together, and Mama put on her courtroom smile. "Lena, how nice to see you. Are you here visiting with the children?"

"Someone has to make sure they're fine." Mrs. Greene stood up. "What do you plan to cook for supper?"

"I'm not cooking," Mama said. "I stopped by Tessie's, and she gave me a nice roast chicken with some sides and a tossed salad."

Mrs. Greene's face scrunched up. Our grandma didn't care much for Mrs. Bledsoe, who ran a soul food restaurant in Alton. She said that the menu was common and catered to white folks who didn't know any better.

"So no home-cooked meal? At all? Not even hot cornbread?" She frowned.

Mama paused, and I knew she was counting to three in her head. "You're welcome to join us."

CHAPTER NINE
Spoiled Supper

Janie, Ellis, and I washed our hands in the hall bathroom before setting the silverware in the dining room. Usually we ate our meals in the kitchen, but there wasn't enough room with Mrs. Greene joining us for supper. Most times, we only came in the dining room to swipe off dust mites and wipe down the glass armoire full of fancy dishes we never used.

Mrs. Greene sat at one end of the table, and Daddy sat at the opposite end. Mama, Ellis, Janie, and I sat in the middle, facing one another.

After we settled in our chairs, Daddy smiled at me. "Sarah, do you want to say the grace?" he asked.

"Can I do the grace tonight?" Ellis asked.

"No," Mama and Daddy replied in unison.

"Let the boy do it," Mrs. Greene said. "It's encouraging to see Jesus in his heart."

Mama gave Daddy a worried glance. "Go ahead, Ellis."

My brother cleared his throat, closed his eyes tight, and clasped his fingers. "Lord, thank you for this supper. Let this food bless our bodies and our sinning souls. Lord, drench us in the blood of your son Jesus to keep us safe from harm. Let him keep us from getting stitches—"

"Ellis, finish the grace with some sense," Mama snapped.

My brother slipped back into prayer mode. "Lord? Bless the humans and creatures at this table. In your name we pray. Amen."

I opened my eyes. Janie's face was turning pink from holding in her laughter, but Mrs. Greene was not amused.

"I hope there's still some time left for this child to come out right." Mrs. Greene frowned at Ellis, who returned the look with a big grin.

Janie couldn't hold it in any longer and let out a snicker.

"What's so funny?" I quietly asked.

"Ellis put Walter under the table," she whispered in my ear, and then beamed as she cut her chicken into bite-size pieces.

"How is the planning going with the Heritage Festival?" Daddy asked Mrs. Greene.

"Everything is just fine," she said. "All of our booths are filled."

"What did the board decide to do with Mrs. Whitney's request?" Mama asked. "I heard she presented a different idea for her booth?"

"Her request came in too late," Mrs. Greene snipped.

I could tell that Mama didn't believe her. "That's unfortunate."

"Robert, when are you going to open your own business?" Mrs. Greene said, completely changing the subject. "You need to have something that's yours. Stop working for other folks."

Daddy worked as a civil engineer in Alton. Mrs. Greene wanted him to be a mortician like Granddaddy Greene, but Daddy didn't have the stomach for it. He always said he would rather deal with bridges than with bodies.

"I'm working on it, Mama," he said. "Things are good right now."

"Delilah, have you divorced or sued anybody this week?" Mrs. Greene asked.

"I haven't yet, but it's only Monday," Mama replied.

"Don't understand why you insist on having that law office. My son can provide for this family. A Greene woman should focus on her children and her husband."

Mama paused, and then smiled sweetly. "I insist on using my law office to help our community. And as you can see, my children and my husband are perfectly fine."

Mrs. Greene huffed and took a sip of her sweet tea, but she didn't say anything else.

We ate the remainder of our meal in silence. We were almost finished eating when, to my horror, I saw Walter climbing the tablecloth. I nudged Janie with my foot. Ellis was too busy sucking the life out of his last chicken bone to even notice.

Crash!

Walter leaped on top of the table, knocking over a glass of sweet tea. Daddy screeched and jumped up from his chair, making it hit the hardwood floor with a loud plop. He tried to catch Walter, but the lizard slipped out of his grasp and raced straight across the table toward Mrs. Greene.

"Run, Walter! Run!" Ellis yelled.

The bearded dragon jumped and took a high dive right into our grandma's lap.

"Ahhhhhhhhhhhh," Mrs. Greene wailed.

Mama dropped her fork with a loud clatter. Janie couldn't contain her giggling and clutched her stomach, gasping for air. I sat frozen in my seat, unable to move.

Mrs. Greene jumped up from her chair and continued to scream at the top of her lungs as Walter dropped to the floor. Ellis disappeared underneath the dining room table, searching for his pet lizard.

Our grandma's face was flushed; her glossy hair bounced with each heavy breath. She put her hand to her chest. "It tried to attack me," she panted. "Some kind of heathen. A soldier of Lucifer."

"It's okay." Daddy rushed over to Mrs. Greene. "It's just Walter. He doesn't bite. He must have gotten out of his cage."

"Ellis!" Mama yelled, her voice laced with anger.

My brother slowly came out from underneath the table, Walter in the crook of his arm.

"What did I tell you about bringing that lizard to supper?" Mama asked.

Mrs. Greene glared at Ellis. "This child is Satan's seed! He needs the wrath of a switch!"

Ellis moved quickly behind Mama. His eyes were wide and scared.

Daddy rubbed Mrs. Greene's shoulders. "Calm down. We'll take care of him. Just take a deep breath."

Mrs. Greene picked up her handkerchief, and Daddy guided her out of the dining room. Mama grabbed Ellis by the elbow, and he yelped. "You are in big trouble, young man. To your room right now."

When our grandma finally calmed down, she left grumbling and in a bad mood. Janie and I sat in the den while Mama and Daddy were upstairs with Ellis. No doubt he was getting a good long talk. My parents didn't use switches, but Mama's lashing words were just as rough.

"I told Ellis to put Walter under the table," Janie said.

"Why did you do that?" I asked.

"He was gonna snitch on us," she said. "You should thank me."

"But now he's in trouble," I said.

"Better him than us."

Even though I didn't like her tactics, Janie had prevented Ellis from telling Mama that we went to Creek Church.

Janie pulled out her phone. "I'm gonna call my mom."

Janie left to go out on the porch, so I went into Mama's office and checked my e-mail. Nothing from Jovita. The disappointment I usually felt from my empty inbox had disappeared. My stomach didn't fill like a bag of gravel. I was now numb to my best friend ignoring me. My mind was too filled up with questions from what I had seen today.

After closing my e-mail, I typed *Are ghosts real?* into the search engine. Out of the millions of hits, I read the top result: *No scientific evidence.*

Later that night, Janie clicked on the nightstand lamp between us.

"Sarah? Are you still awake?"

"What do you want?"

"Do you believe in that curse?" she asked.

"I thought you didn't believe it," I said.

"I didn't say I did. But there was something odd

about that boy. Do you think he was one of those haint things?"

"Go to sleep, Janie."

She clicked off the lamp, leaving my spaceship clock to be the only source of weak light. I continued to stare at the ceiling, my mind racing with questions. Had I seen shadows in front of that dead oak tree? Were we now cursed? Was that strange boy a haint? Or something else? Anything could seem like magic until it was explained. I knew there had to be some kind of explanation, but right now I couldn't think of a single one.

CHAPTER TEN

Cursed

The next morning I left Janie in my room burrowed deep under the covers and had breakfast with my parents.

"Get a good night's sleep?" Mama asked.

"I slept okay," I said.

Ellis hadn't snitched on us, but I still felt guilty about going to Creek Church. I was worried about our little trip and Janie's sticky fingers coming back to haunt us, literally.

Daddy poured me a half cup of coffee. Mama wouldn't let him give me a full cup yet. After adding hot water, a scoop of sugar, and a dollop of cream, I closed my eyes and enjoyed the warm rush. Even though it was watered down, I loved how coffee woke up my brain.

"You're still watching the *History of the Solar System*?" Daddy asked.

"Yep," I replied.

"Excited about the science conference?" Mama gave me half of her bagel, and I let my spoonful of peanut butter ooze over the crunchy crust.

"I can't wait. I have so many questions," I said.

Daddy walked to the sink and washed out his coffee cup. "I need to confirm our reservation at the hotel. Looking forward to a weekend with my best girl."

"Hey, I thought I was your best girl?" Mama punched him playfully in the shoulder.

"You're the first lady in my life." Daddy kissed Mama on the nose, and she giggled like a teenager.

"Can we go to Alton on Saturday?" I asked. "Janie wants to buy more nail polish."

"Sure," Daddy said. "Maybe while we're there we can catch that asteroid disaster movie your brother wants to see."

"I'm not sure if that's a good choice," Mama said.

"Is Ellis on punishment?" I asked.

"No," Daddy said. "He now understands some pranks shouldn't be played. Just keep an eye on him. I don't want him getting into any more trouble."

I wanted to tell my parents it wasn't Ellis they should be worried about. Janie was the one who was looking for trouble. I wondered if I should just tell them about what had happened. How Janie made me take her to Creek Church. I wanted to tell Mama about the strange boy, too. What if he was homeless and hungry? Mama would know how to help him. But then I would get in trouble, and Mama might reconsider having put me in charge. My summer would be spent at Mrs. Greene's house, doing chores in the hot sun. No, I couldn't tell them. I would just have to keep my cousin away from that place.

"Sarah, you can do this, right?" Mama asked. "Watch over both Ellis and Janie?"

"Yes, I can do it," I said.

After my parents left for work, I cleaned up the kitchen and then settled in to watch another *History of the Solar System* episode. I snuggled deep into the couch as I learned how the asteroid belt formed between Mars and Jupiter.

Ellis bounded down the stairs and came into the den. I paused the TV. "Don't ask me to fry an egg. Cereal is on the table for your convenience."

"I know," he grumbled.

My brother ate his breakfast and unpacked

another model car set while I finished watching the *History of the Solar System* episode.

I opened up my thick book about the Cassini spacecraft voyage to Saturn. Most people know about the rings, but the planet is so much more. Saturn was Earth's protector, slinging asteroids away from our path and allowing life to evolve and thrive—well at least some life, since an asteroid did wipe out the dinosaurs. A season on Saturn lasts about seven Earth years. I imagined a seven-year summer filled with humid days and strawberry ice cream. It wouldn't be a true summer since we would have to go to school, but I would enjoy the long hours filled with sunshine. But that would mean seven-year winters, too. Cold nights and bare trees. The average human would get to see each of our seasons maybe three times in their lifetime, if they were lucky.

I flipped the pages to my favorite photo, where the Cassini spacecraft, almost nine hundred million miles away, was positioned under the rings of Saturn and showed Earth as a distant pale sphere, its moon only a faint shadow.

The photo was titled *The Day the Earth Smiled*. It reminded me of a similar photo taken by another spacecraft, *Voyager 1*, right before it left our solar system at the request of astronomer Carl Sagan. Earth was barely visible, a small faded speck. Dr. Sagan had said that everyone we've ever loved, everyone we've ever known, all that we've ever been as a human species had lived on a pale blue dot in the vastness of space.

Maybe one day we would find life on another planet or a moon. Maybe in our solar system or in another galaxy. Another intelligent species. We couldn't be the only ones. I needed to believe we weren't alone in the universe.

I settled deeper into the couch and spent the next hour reading about Cassini's discoveries of Saturn.

Ellis and I both jumped when we heard Janie's screams.

I knew this morning bliss wouldn't last.

I narrowed my eyes at Ellis. "I swear, if you put Walter in her bed, I'm calling Mama."

"I didn't do nothing," Ellis said. "Sounds like she's having a nervous breakdown."

We scrambled up the stairs and found Janie still in her nightgown, gaping at the window. I hadn't opened the curtains because I didn't want the bright sunshine to disturb her. Now the curtains were wide open, and Ellis and I stared at the window.

A message was scrawled across the pane in mud.

TAKE IT BACK

Janie's face was scrunched up as if she had smelled the foulest rotten egg in history. I slowly moved toward the window, staring at the message. The words were written from the outside. Small block letters in reddish-brown mud made by a fingertip. How had someone gotten up to the second level of our house? I looked out the window but didn't see anything suspicious. The hydrangea bushes looked fine, and the ivy trellis looked undisturbed.

Janie stormed toward Ellis and dug her finger into his chest. "I know you're trying to scare me about that stupid curse, but it won't work!"

The cameo. We had received a warning. Three simple words. *Take it back.* Or else.

Ellis knew Janie had taken the cameo. Was this my brother's idea of a prank? He was with us at supper and then in his room all night. Maybe he could have sneaked outside later, but that seemed doubtful. I couldn't see Ellis pulling something like this off.

"Where is the cameo?" I asked.

"She probably put it with her secret stash." Ellis looked under Janie's bed and pulled out her pink backpack.

Janie pushed Ellis, and my brother hit the floor with a loud thud. "Don't touch my stuff!"

I bent down beside him. "Are you okay?"

He blinked several times. "She just tried to kill me!"

"Serves you right," Janie said. "You touch my stuff again, and you'll be dead for real."

"Murder is a felony!" Ellis said. "I'm telling Mama!"

"Stop it!" I yelled at both of them. "We need to figure this out."

Janie sat on the edge of her bed, gripping her backpack. Ellis stood up and rolled his shoulders, giving our cousin the stank eye.

"Let me see the cameo," I demanded.

Janie frowned but unzipped the front pocket of her backpack and pulled it out. I took the cameo and examined it. There was nothing special or unusual about it. It was just a discarded, dirty piece of jewelry.

I looked back up at the window. Who wrote that message? I thought of the strange boy we had seen at

Creek Church, and a small, cold twinge traveled up my back.

"I hate to break this to y'all, but I didn't have anything to do with this," Ellis said. "A haint wrote that message. You didn't listen to me. I *told* you not to take anything. Now you're cursed."

"I'm not cursed!" Janie yelled.

"You better take that jewelry back before it gets worse," Ellis said.

"We don't know who left that message, but there's no way some haint wrote it. How can they write anything? They're not alive," I said.

"Jasper believes this curse is the real deal," Ellis said. "He's seen too much working for that root witch at the Train Depot."

My brother's words triggered something. Did Jasper know we had gone to Creek Church? If anyone wanted us to believe in the curse, then it would be him.

CHAPTER ELEVEN

Seed of Doubt

Ellis went downstairs to call Jasper and ask him to come over. Janie left and went to the bathroom to wash her face and brush her teeth.

I stood in the middle of my room and stared at the message on the window. Ellis believed ghosts had come to our house and written those words, but that was preposterous.

Last summer, Daddy and I watched *Contact*, one of his favorite movies. It centered on a woman named Dr. Arroway, an astrophysicist who traveled through space and time to meet aliens. In one scene, Dr. Arroway talked about the basic scientific principle of Occam's razor, which states the simplest explanation is usually the right one.

A more simple explanation for the message was that Jasper had ridden over here on his bike, climbed up the ivy trellis, and written the message himself. Jasper was real. Haints were not.

Although . . . the trellis was frail and probably couldn't hold Jasper's weight. And why didn't we hear anything last night? Did Jasper even know we had gone to Creek Church? The simple explanation was getting more complicated.

I was trying to convince myself that everything could be explained, but deep down, there was still a tiny seed of doubt, and it was growing.

In another scene from *Contact*, when Dr. Arroway returned from space, no one believed she had traveled across the galaxy and met another intelligent species. Even the principle of Occam's razor made it seem like she was making it all up. Dr. Arroway couldn't prove it or explain it, but she held fast to her belief. She had met the aliens, and they were real.

I was so confused. I didn't know what to believe anymore. Too many things were happening that I couldn't easily clarify.

When Janie came back into my bedroom, she had changed into a yellow halter top and cutoff jeans.

"Sarah, I think you're right," she said. "Jasper

may be behind all of this, but I still think Ellis had something to do with it too. He's got a sneaky streak in him, and he wants revenge on me. This is why I hate boys."

I pulled out a T-shirt and khaki shorts from the dresser. "My brother doesn't have enough imagination for this. I think Jasper is trying to prove a point." I took off my housecoat and put on my bra. I was so wrapped up in theory, I didn't care if Janie stared.

"What about that boy we saw?" she asked. "Do you think we need to tell Jasper and Ellis about him?"

"He was probably just some kid from the trailer park," I said. "Creek Church isn't that far from there."

"Maybe." Janie pulled her braids over to one shoulder and studied the nail polish on her thumb. "I'm going downstairs to eat breakfast. Hurry up and fix your hair. We need to be ready when Jasper gets here, and he better be in the mood for talking."

When she left the room, I noticed the strap of Janie's backpack peeking out from underneath the bed. I stared at it as I pulled on my shorts. It taunted me as I put my hair into two French braids.

Who else would get a kick out of this whole thing?

My cousin loved trouble. She had convinced Ellis to bring Walter to supper. She complained about being bored. Maybe *she* wrote the message? She could have easily snuck out of the house. She was definitely light enough to climb up the ivy trellis.

I also hadn't forgotten the way she came down from Mrs. Greene's attic with that smirk on her face. What else was she hiding in that pink backpack of hers?

I pushed up the bedspread and pulled out the backpack. The zipper made a loud *zmpff* noise. I found the MLK church fan, celebrity magazines, and nail polish. I also found a small silver hand with a blue eye. The same one showcased at Mrs. Whitney's gift shop. How had Janie taken one of these?

Light footsteps traveled up the stairs, and I quickly crammed everything back into the backpack, zipped it as fast as I could, and shoved it under Janie's bed.

"What's taking you so long?" My cousin appeared in the doorway.

I tried to remove the guilt from my face. "I'm ready."

"I came to get the cameo." Janie reached under her bed and retrieved it from the front pocket of her backpack.

I followed Janie downstairs in relief.

• • •

It didn't take Jasper long to arrive. He cruised down our street and swooped into the driveway. He jumped off his bike with wheels spinning and bounded up the porch steps.

"Where is the message?" Jasper panted.

He followed us upstairs to my bedroom and stood in front of my window. I studied his face. Jasper didn't seem amused; he looked afraid.

"This is what happens when folks don't listen to me," Ellis said.

"So what do you have to say for yourself?" Janie came up beside Jasper and put her hand on her hip. "Proud of your little handiwork? Guess what, though? You didn't scare me."

Jasper looked down at her, his eyebrows furrowed together in confusion. "I didn't do this."

"Stop playing games," Janie said. "We know Ellis told you that we went to Creek Church."

"I didn't tell him anything," Ellis said. "He just found out when I called him this morning."

I went and stood on the other side of Jasper. "You didn't know anything about the cameo?" I asked him.

"I have no idea what's going on. But this right here?" He pointed to the window. "This is bad news. What did you do?"

Janie and I looked at each other. The smirk on her face instantly faded, and I felt a slight queasiness in my stomach.

What had Mrs. Whitney told Jasper? I thought of all the creepy things we had seen at the back of her gift shop: bags of herbs, spooky dolls, and the tower of silver hands. I also remembered Mrs. Whitney's words. *Don't mess with the spirit world, and it won't mess with you.*

"Did you take something from Creek Church?" Jasper asked.

Janie pulled the cameo out of her pocket and gave it to him. "It's just a piece of junk jewelry. What does it matter?"

"It matters to the haints," Jasper said. "They don't like it."

"So you really believe a haint wrote this?" I asked.

"Mrs. Whitney told me that Creek Church is a sacred place. Frozen in time. Nothing should be moved or taken away."

"I tried to warn them." Ellis sneered at Janie.

"Shut up," she snapped.

I sat down at my desk to think. I glanced at my astronomy books, but I knew I wouldn't find any answers there.

It was clear that Jasper hadn't written the message, and the way my cousin was acting, it didn't seem likely that she had written it either. It could only mean one thing.

"We saw a boy at Creek Church," I blurted out. "About eight years old. Dark skinned. Torn-up clothes. Bare, muddy feet. Jasper, have you ever seen a kid like this around the trailer park? Maybe he's homeless?"

"Not many kids live in the trailer park anymore," Jasper said, his voice quaking.

I wanted to ask him about the dead oak tree and the shadows, but the way Jasper kept staring at the words on the window made me pause. He was looking more and more afraid.

"You have to take the cameo back," Jasper whispered.

"You should come with us," Janie said. "Both of you."

Ellis frowned. "Didn't you hear what he said? He didn't say *we* should go. He said *you* should go."

"Too scared?" Janie sneered.

"I ain't scared." Ellis pulled out his prized slingshot from his pocket. "I know how to protect myself."

Janie laughed. "You think that thing is gonna protect us?"

I stood up from my desk. Of course. Janie had taken something from Creek Church, and to break the curse she must return the cameo to the graveyard. I quickly had the sinking feeling that if we didn't, something else could happen, and I didn't want to find out what. There were already too many odd things going on.

"If going back will get rid of the curse, let's just do it so we can get out of this mess," I said.

"So you'll come with us?" Janie asked Jasper.

Jasper was silent for several seconds, and then Ellis groaned.

"You don't have to come," I told Jasper. "This is Janie's problem. She needs to deal with it."

"I'll go with you," Jasper said.

"Ellis, you're coming too," I said.

"Why I gotta go with y'all?" he whined.

"We need to stay together."

Janie grabbed the cameo from Jasper. "Let's go."

CHAPTER TWELVE

The Black Tree

The heat from the asphalt rose up in shimmers as we walked down Hardeman Road. The sunlight on my hair made my scalp itch. The humidity was heavy in the air, but the goose bumps remained on my skin.

Janie tugged my T-shirt, her face serious. "You think going back will help?"

"We wouldn't have to go back if you had listened to me," Ellis said.

"I didn't take anything; I found it." Janie pushed her chin up in the air and closed her eyes to the sun.

"Will you stop saying that? You didn't find anything. You took it. Just like you took the church fan and that creepy—" I stopped myself. I couldn't reveal that I had seen the silver hand from Mrs. Whitney's gift shop. If I did, then she would know I had been snooping in her backpack. I trotted up between Jasper and Ellis to get away from her.

"Most ghosts don't know they're dead," Jasper said.

"That doesn't seem fun," Ellis said. "To be dead and not know it."

"Mrs. Whitney says this whole town got a reckoning with the dead left at Creek Church."

"You mean the ones in the graveyard?" I asked.

"No," Jasper said. "Others who are trapped there. They can't leave. They're bound to that place because of unfinished business. Mrs. Whitney says it's up to their blood kin to free them."

"What does that even mean?" Janie asked. "When you're dead, you're dead."

"I wouldn't stay here. I would be up in heaven, chilling. Eating all the fried eggs I wanted," Ellis said.

Jasper glanced at us. "Mrs. Whitney is on a mission to free every restless spirit in Warrenville. Folks in town are interested too. She's taking appointments."

"Appointments?" I asked. "For what?"

"Spiritual problems. She meets with her clients in a back room. She helps them out."

Maybe that explained all of those things Mrs. Whitney had in her gift shop.

"Are the appointments free?" I asked.

"She takes donations," Jasper said. "She has different types of payment plans."

"Sounds like a scam artist to me," Janie said.

I wondered if Mama knew about this. Even though she thought Mrs. Whitney was eccentric, Mama wouldn't like it if she found out that Mrs. Whitney was feeding on superstitions and taking money from hardworking folks.

But what if Mrs. Whitney was right? What if Warrenville did have a haint problem? I had seen enough strange things happen that my seed of doubt had grown roots. I couldn't explain what Janie and I had seen, and now I was going back to Creek Church, the origin of everything, because I had a tiny shred of belief that the curse might be real, and I didn't want to take any chances.

We turned off Hardeman Road onto Linnard Run. Nothing had changed from yesterday. The broken chain was still on the ground, tire tracks were still pressed into the dried mud, and trash still lay scattered in the bushes. This time I didn't bother looking at the NO TRESPASSING sign.

As we walked down the dirt road, I searched the woods for any sign of movement. At the dead end, we saw the mossy stone steps shaded in darkness. Cold sweat prickled at the base of my back, and my heartbeat pounded in my ears.

Janie pressed through the weeds and stood on the steps with Jasper right behind her. "The graveyard is farther back in the woods. That's where I found the cameo."

Ellis pulled out his slingshot and searched for rocks. I remained still, trying to slow down my heartbeat. Despite the heat, I was shivering. My nervous system sensed something bad was in the air. Something dangerous. My body was telling me to run.

I really didn't want to go to the graveyard because I would have to pass the dead oak tree again, but I needed to make sure Janie put the cameo back in its place. I grabbed my brother's hand, but he wouldn't budge from the dirt road.

"Come on, Ellis," I said.

"I couldn't find any good rocks to protect us," he said. "We should stay here and just wait for them."

"We need to stick together, just in case," I said.

Ellis positioned his slingshot in front of him as a shield as we continued deeper into the woods.

"I thought you said you couldn't find any rocks?"

"I always bring backup." He held out his palm to reveal three tiger's eye marbles. "I don't know if these will work, but they're from my special collection."

We crept past the dead oak tree. No shadows. I grabbed my brother's hand again and headed eastward to the graveyard.

We found Jasper and Janie in front of a tombstone. She held the cameo in her hand.

"How do we know if this will break the curse?" Janie asked.

"Because that's what Mrs. Whitney says," Jasper replied.

"So we're gonna believe a possible scam artist?" Janie frowned.

"You saw that message. Also, this is the only thing we *can* do," I said. "Do you have any other ideas?"

"Do it," Ellis said.

Janie pushed away some old leaves and put the cameo back in the dirt. I rubbed my arms, hoping to remove the shivers.

Jasper bent down to examine the tombstone. "That cameo may have belonged to a relative paying her respects to this grave."

"It could have belonged to anyone," Janie said.

"We're done here. We should leave," Jasper urged.

I didn't realize I had been holding my breath. I let out a deep sigh. "I hope this fixes everything."

A crow cawed, and Ellis pointed his slingshot in its direction. The sunlight peeked through the foliage. I focused on the black tree, dark against the bright green woods.

A gust of wind whipped through the graveyard and knocked Ellis down to the ground; it hit my face, and faint whispers filled the woods.

Ellis staggered to his feet and aimed his sling-shot toward the trees. "Do you hear that? It's coming from up there!"

We gathered in a circle with our backs to one another, gaping at the trees. The whispers rose with the wind, hissing like angry snakes. We moved closer together until the wind weakened and the noises stopped. Janie gripped my hand. The air suddenly grew colder, and our breath curled out from our mouths in cloudy puffs. We stood still, afraid to move.

"What's happening?" Janie asked in a small voice.

Jasper put his finger to his lips to silence her. Across from us in the graveyard, the branches of the black tree creaked and swayed. Dark shadows, like wisps of smoke, filtered out of the trunk and hovered above the dead branches.

"Are you seeing this?" Ellis's voice was high and squeaky.

The shadows broke apart into several globs of inky blackness and then began to take shape into human form. Two arms. Two legs. I hadn't been imagining things. I had seen this yesterday. It was happening again.

They thinned and grew taller than anything human. The shadows twisted around the trunk and gazed at us with silver eyes. They settled in front of the black tree. One of them pointed at us as it hissed.

Jasper and Ellis were the first to run. Janie and I fled behind them. The woods blurred as we zigzagged back to the church. We jumped up onto the stone slab and raced down the steps. I didn't turn to look behind me, afraid to see if the shadows were chasing us. We shoved ourselves through the bushes and ran down the dirt road until we were in the safety of the sunlight.

We panted at the entrance of Linnard Run. Nothing had followed us, and no shadows were in sight.

Everything was calm.

Janie punched Jasper in the arm. "Why did you leave us like that?"

Jasper didn't say anything. Was he shocked? Scared? Maybe he was both. I know I was.

"Don't get mad at him," Ellis said. "You saw what happened. We were about to be haint food."

I couldn't deny it. What we had seen was as real as the sun, the stars, and the planets in our solar system. Those shadows were physical things, and they weren't human. I didn't need any more theories. No more explanations. Creek Church was haunted.

CHAPTER THIRTEEN

Dark History

Jasper's trailer had pale blue shutters and sat on four concrete blocks. Next to a picnic table, a clothesline sagged low with laundry. I tried not to stare at the underwear blowing in the wind. In the small yard were several birdbaths. The last time I visited I had counted seven, but I think Jasper's mama added a couple more since then.

We traveled past the trailer to an open field and sat under a weeping willow tree. The long branches rustled in the summer breeze, and the leaves provided a curtain of shade. Jasper fetched us a bowl of blackberries from his refrigerator, and Ellis immediately dug in; he smashed several of them into his mouth. After watching him do this three times, I took the bowl away from him.

"Hey!" he protested. "Give that back."

"You're eating too many blackberries. You're going to get sick," I warned.

Janie sat next to me, her braids hiding her face. She stayed silent and peeled nail polish off her big toe. Jasper twirled blades of grass in front of him.

"Now that the cameo is back in the graveyard, everything should be okay, right?" I asked.

Ellis pointed at Janie. "Wouldn't even have to deal with none of this if you had just listened to me."

Janie smacked his hand down. "Leave me alone."

I glowered at Janie. My brother was right. She had created this whole mess. Now I had uncovered something I didn't want to believe but couldn't deny after our experiences yesterday and today. Ghosts were real, and this town was cursed with them.

"Those shadows? The ones that came from the black tree? They were the same ones I saw yesterday," I said.

"Those must be the restless spirits," Jasper said. "Torn from the living world in a painful way, unable to move on."

Daddy had told us about Warrenville's dark history. Back in the day, any member of the black community could be killed without punishment. No judge. No jury. Killed without cause. Most of the time it was because of false rumors. Other times, a blood sport. We were killed because we were in the wrong place at the wrong time. We were killed because we didn't stay in our place. We were killed for wanting a better future. We were killed for having the audacity to even exist. It was true that Warrenville had changed over the years, but its past would stay the same. Nothing could ever change that.

"So those haints are trapped there? They can't leave?" Janie asked.

"That's what Mrs. Whitney says," Jasper said.

"You say that the ghosts usually want something. Unfinished business. Maybe they want vengeance," I said. "Or justice."

We all stared at one another. We knew those spirits wouldn't find who they were looking for. As the haints dwelled at Creek Church, the folks who had killed them had lived long lives. Never punished. Never prosecuted. Unscathed by their crimes. Justice wasn't available to the haints. Not anymore.

"So did we stir up a different curse?" I asked.

"We took back the cameo," Jasper said. "The haints should respect that. But—"

"Will they come to our house again?" Ellis asked.

Jasper stayed silent for a few moments. "There's no reason for them to bother you anymore."

"You don't seem so sure. And what about the boy?" Janie asked. "We didn't see him."

Yesterday the boy looked so young and fragile standing on the stone steps. He looked alive and real. But I also remember how he made me feel. Unsettled. The sunlight had curved around him. I was glad we hadn't seen him today, because it would have confirmed he wasn't a boy at all.

"We've done all we can." I stood up and brushed the grass off my shorts with trembling hands. My nervous system was telling me to go someplace safe.

"We need to go home," I said.

Ellis and Jasper got up, but Janie didn't move. She sat with her arms crossed.

"Janie, get up. Let's go," I said with irritation.

She rose off the ground and tossed her braids over her shoulder. "So that's it? We're going to forget this ever happened?"

"What do you want us to do?" I asked.

"We saw ghosts!" Janie shook her hands in the air. "Don't you think we should tell someone?"

"Tell who?" Ellis asked. "I ain't telling Mama nothing about this."

"We're done with that place," I said.

"But what about the little boy? Didn't you say he could be lost or homeless?"

"I don't think we can help him," I said.

"So what—we leave that little boy out there in the woods by himself?" Janie said. "You just want to hide in your boring books and study stupid science all day."

Anger flared through me. I pushed Jasper out of the way and shoved my finger hard into Janie's chest. "You should be scared. Did you see those shadows? The way they fell from that dead tree? The way those haints hissed at us? If that little boy is hanging around there, you can best believe he doesn't need our help."

Janie twisted her mouth into a frown but stayed silent. She knew I was right.

"That place is off-limits. Now we know why. We're staying away from it. You're only here for twelve more days. If you wanna be haunted by a haint, then that's your business. Go by yourself. Leave me and Ellis out of it."

She scowled at me. "Fine. Keep your little ghost-country town. See if I care," she taunted. Then she marched out of the field.

I turned to Jasper. "I need you to keep this between us. Don't tell Mrs. Whitney what happened."

"Okay," he said. "But she may be able to help you."

"If taking the cameo back fixes everything, then we don't need anyone's help."

Mrs. Whitney had told us not to mess with the spirit world, but we had anyway. Lesson learned. I wouldn't be messing with them ever again.

"Don't tell anyone else, either," I added. "We don't need our parents finding out about this."

As soon as we got back home, I went into the backyard and took Mama's garden hose to wash off the message from my bedroom window. As the muddy letters dripped down the glass pane, so too did my questions and doubt; my body sighed in relief.

I would never go to Creek Church again.

CHAPTER FOURTEEN
Thicker than Water

Over the next three days, Janie gave me the silent treatment. Every time I tried to start a conversation, she ignored me and hid her face behind one of Aunt Gina's celebrity magazines or played on her phone. No longer squeamish or scared of the bearded dragon, Janie hung out in Ellis's room and held Walter like a baby. Despite my brother's pleas to feed Walter crickets, Janie insisted on only giving him kale and carrots.

I hadn't confronted my cousin about taking the silver hand from Mrs. Whitney's gift shop. She never brought it out of her backpack. The only thing she would take out of her so-called purse was nail polish for her daily pedicure.

I tried to return to my summer routine and read my Cassini book, but Saturn's moons had lost their appeal. I didn't care that Mimas was one of the most battered moons in our solar system or that Titan had formed rivers and lakes from a millennia of methane rain. No matter how hard I tried to go into my astronomy bubble, I found myself wondering about the strange boy.

I continued to share breakfast with Mama and drink coffee with Daddy. I didn't tell them about Creek Church, and the guilt still lay heavy on my conscience. But what could I do? They wouldn't believe me if I told them I had seen haints float down from a dead tree.

Ellis kept to his model car project, and Janie and Mrs. Taylor established a closer bond, watching housewives backstab each other on reality TV.

Several times I went into Mama's office and checked my e-mail. Still nothing from Jovita. One day I typed a long message telling her everything. I told her about Janie and her sticky fingers and how she hated our small town. I told her about Creek Church and how haints were trapped in a forgotten place from Warrenville's history. I shared my theories about the strange boy and that maybe he wasn't a boy at all.

I read through the e-mail and hovered over the send button. Then I remembered how Jovita had gone to Yvonne's party without me. How she had ignored me all summer. She never responded to my other e-mails, so she probably wouldn't read this one either. Wiping a tear from my eye, I slowly deleted each word until there was nothing left but an empty screen.

That night I went to sleep and dreamed of haints with silver eyes watching over me.

On Saturday we piled into Daddy's SUV to go to the Alton Mall. In the backseat, I squished myself near the window and listened to Ellis and Janie discuss Walter's diet.

"I think we should make Walter a vegetarian," Janie said.

"Crickets are insects not animals," Ellis said.

"But crickets are nasty," Janie complained.

"Cockroaches are actually better," Ellis said.

Janie scrunched up her face. "Even more disgusting."

When we got inside the mall, Daddy took Ellis to the video game store, and Mama wanted to shop for a blouse at her favorite boutique. I asked to tag along, even if it meant Mama would buy me another training bra, but she had other plans.

"Sarah, take Janie to the makeup store or that accessory place. They may have her nail polish."

Janie frowned. "I can find it by myself."

Mama shook her head as if she was rejecting a plea bargain at the Fairfield County courthouse. This was non-negotiable.

"Sarah will go with you." Mama looked at her watch. "I'll meet you ladies in the food court in about an hour."

After Mama left us to fend for ourselves, we walked in silence. Creek Church was the only bond we had in common. And that wasn't anything I wished to share with anyone.

The mall wasn't crowded because it was summer and the university students were gone, but there was still a buzz. Little kids screamed as they rode on a small carousel in the play area. Older kids sat on the benches, people watching and gossiping. The last time I had gone to the Alton Mall was with Jovita. Mama had dropped us off, and we had spent our allowance at Candy Unlimited and shared a milkshake in the food court. Jovita had told me about her secret crush on Joseph Conway. That seemed like a lifetime ago.

"This mall is a joke," Janie said.

"Maybe before you leave we can go to Atlanta," I said. "They have some fun stores."

Janie sucked her teeth and tossed her braids over her shoulder. "Mom is coming back for me next weekend. We won't have time."

I knew Aunt Gina called Janie every night. No doubt my cousin was still complaining about how much she hated staying with us. But Janie never talked to anyone else, and I wondered if she even had a best friend. It didn't seem like it. Maybe that was another thing we had in common.

"Did Aunt Gina finish her screen tests yet?"

"She has a big audition on Monday," Janie said. "It's only a matter of time before she's a movie star, and we'll be living in a mansion in Hollywood."

"You'll be a celebrity daughter like you always wanted," I added. "But what about your friends in Chicago? Won't you miss them?"

Janie fiddled with her braids. "Not really."

We walked again in silence. I didn't feel like trying to get closer to Janie, even though as a cousin I should have. I wasn't sure what to talk to her about. This would probably be our only time to spark another connection with each other. When she came back next summer, a whole year would be between us. A wider gap to cross.

I stopped in front of the Accessory Alice store. "This is the store Mama was talking about."

Janie strolled in, but I came to a halt at the entrance. Jovita was standing by a display case of earrings. She still looked the same. Deep, dark skin like Mama. Long straight hair pulled back in a simple ponytail.

Jovita was with Yvonne and two other girls. Ones who loved to torture me at school. The three were known as the Jones Girls because they were related in the way families in Alton and Warrenville tended to be. They shared the same light skin and long brown hair. Except Yvonne and Lola were tall and skinny like skeletons, and Sheree was curvy and wore a real bra. They had on matching skirts and tops, which made them look like evil triplets.

When Jovita finally saw me, a look of shame spread across her face. She had been caught in Accessory Alice with my bullies.

"Hi, Sarah," she said.

"When did you get back into town?" I asked.

"Late last night," she said slowly. "I was too tired to call you."

Lola and Sheree sneered as they judged me from

head to toe. I'm sure they didn't approve of my *Hidden Figures* T-shirt, wrinkled shorts, and faded sneakers. Yvonne gave me a she-wolf grin. She was captain of Team Terror. She taunted me in homeroom. She made fun of the way I talked—too much like a white girl. She picked at the way I dressed—too much like a country boy. Mama said Yvonne only did this because she was jealous, but I knew better. Sometimes girls were mean because they wanted to be.

Janie came up beside me and made her rotten-egg face. Within seconds, she could tell these girls weren't my friends.

"We're picking out earrings," Yvonne said. "For Jovita's birthday party."

"So you're still having your party?" I asked.

"I forgot to tell you," she said. "I've been so busy."

"I don't see how you could be busy in this cramped-up, boring place," Janie said.

"Who are you?" Sheree asked.

"I'm Janie, and I don't live here."

"Where you from, then?" Lola asked, annoyance lacing her voice.

"Chicago," Janie replied.

Sheree rolled her eyes and popped her gum. "I've been to Chicago. It ain't all that."

"You look like you're in one of those girl gangs with those fuzzy prison braids," Yvonne said. "Hope you don't plan on robbing this store." The other Jones Girls laughed, but Jovita stayed quiet.

"There's nothing in this place I want," Janie said. "You simple country birds should thank me. You can keep all this cheap mess. It matches your tacky outfits."

Yvonne balled up her hands at her side, and moved toward my cousin, but Jovita quickly jumped between them.

"No need for a scene in a public place. She's already over there watching us." Jovita pointed to an older white woman behind the cash register.

"Y'all gonna buy something or not?" She narrowed her eyes at us. "No loitering."

Jovita cleared her throat. "I'm going to buy these earrings." She showed the woman a pair of earrings in her hands.

"Go ahead and bring them up to the counter," the woman said with an ugly tone in her voice. "You need to make your purchase so you can move along. Don't make me call security."

Jovita glanced at us. "Yes, ma'am."

Lola and Sheree followed her to the sales counter,

but Yvonne lingered behind, a cruel smile plastered to her face.

"You better hope I don't see you around here again," she warned Janie.

Janie grabbed my arm. "Let's go."

We turned and walked out of the store. My hands trembled, the embarrassment burning across my cheeks. Jovita hadn't invited me to her thirteenth birthday party. Worst of all, she'd left me to become friends with those awful girls.

We took the escalator down, and when we got off, I sat on an empty bench. Janie sat beside me. "Are you okay?"

I blinked several times. Jovita had ended our friendship at the Alton Mall. I wanted to cry, but I was also surprised Janie had stood up for me. She didn't have to do that. I knew she was still mad at me about Creek Church, but she came to my defense with the Jones Girls. Maybe this is what they mean when they say blood is thicker than water. Today I liked Janie more than any of my training bras.

"Who cares about Jovita," Janie said. "She has bad taste. In earrings and friends."

I laughed a little, and Janie smiled at me. Maybe the space between us wasn't so big after all.

"I can't believe Jovita is hanging with the Jones Girls. I thought she was my best friend."

"Best friends don't act like that," Janie said.

"Thanks for helping me out with Yvonne," I said. "She hates me."

"She needs to hate herself for dressing like that in public. That country bird has no style whatsoever." Janie stood up from the bench. "Where's that other store? We got one in Chicago so I know they'll have my stuff."

I took her to the makeup store, and Janie found her nail polish. She even talked me into getting a bottle. A bright summer red.

When we met up with Mama at the food court, Janie and I shared chili cheese fries. Mama showed us her new blouse, and we all laughed at Ellis's antics when he explained the plot of his newest video game. It felt good to laugh. Good to forget about Jovita and the Jones Girls. I didn't have a best friend anymore, but at least I had my family.

CHAPTER FIFTEEN
Night Visitor

Rain soaked Warrenville like a drowned rat, causing Missionary Creek to swell into a baby river. Beaverdam Trailer Park had some minor flooding, but Jasper let us know he was okay. He told Ellis the field behind his house looked like a lake. The lightning got so bad that we didn't even go to church. Mrs. Greene called and asked why we weren't sitting in the pews. Despite my grandma's foretelling of Jesus cleansing the earth with rain, the weather forecast promised a clear sky for the Fourth of July fireworks.

Over the next couple of days, the rain held steady, and Mama forced us to stay in the house. I was happy because it meant I could binge-watch the rest of the *History of the Solar System* episodes. Janie whined of boredom, but she entertained herself with pedicures and played video games with Ellis. Sometimes she stayed upstairs, reading magazines and playing on her phone. Even though she had stood up for me in front of Jovita and the Jones Girls, we hadn't said much else to each other.

I was having nightmares. Sometimes I woke up in a cold sweat, a scream at the back of my throat. Other times I dreamed of following the strange boy through the woods and getting lost in the mist. The dead oak tree with shadows slinking down from its branches was always there. I didn't tell anyone about these disturbing dreams. I only wished they would go away.

Tonight was no different. I was in my bed, staring at the ceiling. Like all the previous nights, I prayed for a few dreamless hours. The sheets were over Janie's head as usual. Her steady breathing signaled she was asleep instead of faking it. I fiddled with my warm sheets and pushed them down with my feet.

Our back porch fixture created a spotlight on the trees. The shadows of branches and leaves moved on my bedroom ceiling in a lazy dance. The wind had strengthened, and the leaves bristled in loud whooshes. Lightning pulsed outside my window. My eyelids began to droop, and I fluffed my pillow into a new shape to doze off when I heard the first tap on my window.

I lay frozen, then quickly snuck a glance at my spaceship clock. It was after midnight.

Another tap.

Someone was throwing small pebbles at the glass. Someone was trying to get my attention.

Two more taps.

I sat up in bed and pulled the sheets off me. Teeth clenched, I placed my bare feet on the floor. After a deep breath, I counted to three and walked to the window.

The trees in the backyard were now calm and still. I squinted into the darkness but couldn't see anything. Maybe I was tired. Maybe my mind was playing tricks on me.

Then another rock hit my window, and I jumped back in surprise. The hairs on the back of my neck stood at attention.

It was then that I saw him. The Creek Church boy stood in a sliver of porch light without casting a shadow.

He had on the same clothes. No shoes. I squinted

as his mouth moved. He was trying to say something, but I couldn't understand him—I was too afraid to focus on anything. He turned to the woods behind him. But just before he reached the edge to enter, he looked back at me. The boy's eyes had changed, a silver glow. In the woods behind him, a sea of eyes shimmered in the dark.

Then he was gone.

My body was covered in cold sweat, and my hands trembled. I rushed to Janie's bed and shook her awake. She mumbled in her sleep and pulled the covers over her head.

"Janie." I shook her again.

"What do you want?"

"The boy is outside," I said.

"What?" Janie rubbed her eyes. "Are you sleep-walking?"

"That boy is here."

Janie bolted up. "The one from Creek Church?"

"Yes. He's one of them, Janie. His eyes, they're—"

We raced back to the window, and I pointed to where I had seen him. There was no one there now. The trees swayed in the wind, a storm was brewing.

"Are you sure you weren't dreaming?" she said. "You've been saying weird things in your sleep."

"He woke me up," I said. "He was throwing rocks at the window."

"I don't like this," she said.

We both jumped when the doorbell rang. Janie's eyes went wide. I slowly opened my bedroom door, and Daddy was in the hall with his robe and house shoes. Mama appeared in her nightgown.

The doorbell kept ringing, as if someone desperately wanted to get inside the house.

Ellis peeked out of his room. "Who's ringing our doorbell like we owe them money?"

"Go back in your room," Mama told him.

"Daddy, we shouldn't open the door," I said.

"Someone may need our help," Daddy replied softly.

Janie, Ellis, and I followed my parents downstairs. Whoever was at the door was now knocking urgently.

I grabbed Daddy's hand. "Don't open it."

He pulled the curtains back in the sidelight window. "It's okay, Sarah. It's just Mrs. Taylor."

Our next-door neighbor stood in front of us in her housecoat, bright pink against her dark skin. Mrs. Taylor's gray hair was in rollers, her frail body wrapped in an old fringe shawl.

"Is everything all right?" Daddy asked.

"Somebody was in my backyard," Mrs. Taylor said. "I couldn't see much. Too many shadows. Has your boy been outside?"

"Ellis?" Daddy looked confused.

Ellis peered behind Mama. "I ain't been outside."

Mrs. Taylor walked inside the foyer. "Someone turned on my motion light."

There was certainty in Mrs. Taylor's eyes. She may have had cataracts, but she was right. She had seen something in her backyard, but it wasn't Ellis. My whole body shivered, and Janie inched closer to me.

"Stella, Ellis has been in the house all night," Mama said.

Mrs. Taylor frowned and put her hand over her heart. "I saw him. He was walking around in the dead of night, so I thought you should know."

"Why don't you let me walk you back to your house?" Daddy took Mrs. Taylor by the arm. "Maybe I can take a look around in your backyard, too."

"No, Daddy!" I blurted out.

"Don't do that, Uncle Robert!" Janie chimed in.

"It'll be fine, Sarah," Daddy said. "I'll be right back."

"We can wait here for you," I said.

Daddy turned to look at Mama. She held a hand to her mouth to stifle a yawn. "I'll make the children some hot cocoa."

"That's a good idea, Mama," Ellis said. "Can you fry me an egg, too?"

"No, you'll be up for the rest of the night."

"What about a sandwich, then?" My brother followed Mama into the kitchen.

Janie and I waited by the door. I didn't want Daddy out in Mrs. Taylor's backyard. What if the haints were still there? I rubbed my hands together in worry. After a few long minutes Daddy came back into the house.

"Did you see anything?" I asked.

Daddy shook his head. "I think Mrs. Taylor may have been half-asleep. The wind is blowing hard tonight. A strong gust probably triggered her motion light."

We went into the kitchen, and Mama poured us each a mug of hot cocoa as she fought off another yawn. "Sarah, I'm going back to bed. I'll let you look after these two."

When Mama left, Janie took a small sip from her mug. "Should we tell Ellis?"

"Tell me what?" Ellis dunked a marshmallow into his cocoa.

"The boy from Creek Church was in our back-yard," I said. "There were some haints, too. With him in the woods."

"He's a haint," Janie said. "Sarah saw his eyes change. He's one of them."

"What?!" Ellis shouted.

"Calm down," Janie said.

"You can't tell me to calm down right after you say haints were outside our house!"

"Daddy checked outside. They're gone now," I said.

Ellis shook his head. "If something happens to me, I swear I'm gonna haunt y'all forever."

"Nobody is getting hurt," I said. "Stop talking like that."

I tried to keep my hands from shaking while we drank the rest of our hot cocoa in silence.

CHAPTER SIXTEEN
A Spiritual Problem

The next day brought blinding sunshine, but it also carried a creepy revelation.

"I have something to show you. You ain't gonna like it," Ellis said, motioning for Janie and me to come out to the porch.

The sun had topped over the trees and bathed the front of our house in a warm glow. I shielded my eyes from the brightness.

Ellis pointed to the far corner of the porch. Next to Mama's pot of marigolds my brother's latest model car lay on top of faded newspaper covered in dried mud. The tires were mashed in and crooked, the hood pushed in as if it had been punched by an angry fist. My stomach bubbled with dread. Janie bent down to inspect it.

"Don't touch it!" Ellis said. "Might be booby-trapped."

"You found it like this?" I asked.

He nodded. "I left it out here to let the paint dry like I always do. Somebody took it on a joyride and messed it all up."

Janie moved forward and examined the car more closely. "Look at this, Sarah."

I squatted down beside her and saw a small muddy handprint. Fingertips pressed flat against the faded newspaper. It was slightly smaller than my hand, like it belonged to a younger kid.

"Ellis come here," I said.

My brother took two steps backward. "Nope. Not interested."

Janie stood up. "I bet it was the boy."

"A haint had my car?" Ellis shook his head.

"It doesn't make any sense. Why would he damage it?" I said. "We should have broken the curse. We put the cameo back."

I rambled down the porch steps and went into the backyard. Ellis and Janie followed.

Mama's tall iris plants were in full bloom and framed a small garden of tomatoes, pole beans, and hot peppers. The ground was muddy from the heavy rains, but there was no doubt someone or something had been here last night. There were footprints everywhere.

I stared up at my bedroom window where I had last seen the strange boy. The boy whose eyes flickered silver in the dark.

Traveling down from the roof, muddy handprints stood stark against the white wood of our house. Bigger than the one we saw on the faded newspaper on the porch. Most of them were underneath my window, overlapping in a chaotic pattern. I couldn't tell if they belonged to one person or thing. My throat felt funny, as if I had swallowed a cold rock.

"Were they trying to get inside?" Ellis asked.

The boy had been trying to get my attention, but why? Was he trying to warn me? What if haints did get inside the house? Would they hurt us? Hurt Mama or Daddy? The thought of haints stalking the hallways had me full-on terrified.

A garden hose could wash this evidence away, but this was a bigger problem. We had awakened something. Something that couldn't be ignored.

"This isn't good," I said.

"We should call Jasper," Janie said. "Maybe he knows what this means."

"Jasper can't help us now," I said. "We need to talk with Mrs. Whitney."

We had to figure out how to stop the spirit world from messing with us.

After telling Mrs. Taylor we were taking a walk down to Town Square, we headed out of my neighborhood to Main Street. Ellis slurped from a cup of fruit cocktail, and Janie complained about the heat and lack of shade. I thought the sun was bright and pleasant, a good break from the heavy rains.

I still tried to think of a reason for the muddy handprints underneath my window, but, unlike when we found the message, I didn't try to justify what had happened with a scientific explanation. The boy was one of the restless spirits. A haint with unfinished business.

When we arrived at the Train Depot, both the gift shop and history center doors were locked, CLOSED signs hanging in the windows. Walking around to the loading dock, we found Jasper surrounded by a heap of new deliveries for the gift shop. He wrestled with the boxes that were probably filled with charms, scary dolls, and more silver hands—things Mrs. Whitney had brought to Warrenville to help. I wondered if anyone else in town had muddy hand-prints left around their house. Do the haints make multiple visits? Would they return to our house? What did they want from us? I had so many questions to ask Mrs. Whitney. She needed to know what we had sparked.

"Is Mrs. Whitney around?" I asked. "We need to talk to her."

Jasper took a handkerchief out of his pocket and wiped the sweat off his forehead. "She's kind of busy right now. She's with a client."

"Do you know when she'll be available? We need to make an appointment as soon as possible," I said.

"We have a spiritual problem," Janie added.

"You think?" Ellis finished his fruit cocktail with a long, noisy slurp and threw it in the trash. "Check this out, Jasper. Haints tried to get inside the house. They wrecked my car."

Jasper's mouth dropped open. "What? Start from the beginning."

We started with last night's visit and what we saw in the backyard, the muddy handprints under my bedroom window, the boy with silver eyes. Jasper's eyes grew wide and scared.

"You definitely need an emergency appointment,"

he said. "But I can't disturb her when she's with a client. You'll have to come back."

"We can't just go inside and wait?" Janie asked.

"Sorry, Mrs. Whitney doesn't like anybody in her shop when she has appointments."

Janie pouted and fanned herself, pulling her halter top away from her skin. "What do we do now? Stay out here and melt?"

"We can walk over to the library and wait," I said. "Maybe I can find some books that will help us."

"Come back in an hour," Jasper said.

The Warrenville public library was next door to the post office in Town Square. It was actually a small ranch house with a wraparound porch. Ms. Bell, the librarian, had once told me that good things come in small packages. The library was only open three days a week, when Ms. Bell came up from Alton. Most of the time she brought all the interlibrary loans I had requested. There weren't many shelves for books, but we had all the current newspapers and magazines. Even one ancient computer.

When we entered the library, Ms. Bell was in her usual spot at the front desk. A stack of books hid her tiny body, but I could see her blond hair piled high on top of her head. She had several pencils sticking out of her bun.

"Good morning, Sarah!" Ms. Bell chimed as she peeked around the stack of books. "You need help finding anything today?"

"We're good, Ms. Bell," I said. We didn't need to spook her out too.

"Come find me if you do." She went into the back office.

There was a low probability that there were books in here that could help us, but I knew it wouldn't hurt to look. Knowledge was power. Even for a spiritual problem, there had to be a solution. And even if Mrs. Whitney was the only person who had the expertise, I still wanted to look for myself.

"Okay, let's see if we can find anything," I said.

"Y'all can look. I'm gonna read some comic books." Ellis left us and went to the stack of new issues on the display counter.

Janie also wandered away from me to the periodicals area. She picked up a thick volume of a glossy fashion magazine and promptly sat down on the floor and started to turn the pages.

I sighed. No one wanted to browse the books. Surprise, surprise.

Walking through the aisles, I looked through my regular stash of science books. Most of them I had already read. Ms. Bell and Mama agreed that I could check out books from the adult side too, so I could read more advanced subjects. It was where I had learned about dark matter, the theory of relativity, and my beloved solar system. A lot of the chapters went over my head, but Mama always said it was good to challenge your mind, and in time things would start to make sense.

Turning down the next aisle, I bent down to a shelf I never gave a second glance to, but now I had a different focus. My fingers dragged over a small section of books, all of them covered with a film of dust. I stared at the labels. Parapsychology. Occultism. Ghosts.

I took each book off the shelf and scanned the pages, but they pertained to otherworldly experiences. Nothing about protection.

Disappointed, I put the books back. I was about to join Janie at the periodicals area when another book caught my eye. Small and thin. The gold lettering on the spine glowed in the dim light. *The Witch's Moons.*

I opened the book and looked at several illustrations of different witches worshiping the moon in different seasons.

A woman with flowing blue hair and dark skin stood in a fur-lined cloak in a field of snow. Her eyes were closed, her chin tilted to the full moon.

I read aloud the words on the page. "'The Ice Moon is the time for new promises.'"

On the following page, a pale woman dressed in gold held glowing orbs of lightning in each of her hands as she praised the Thunder Moon. I thought of all the summer storms we'd had in the last week. The bright lightning that lit up my bedroom and the crackling thunder that rumbled in my chest.

I read the snippets for each moon. The Sugar Moon. The Flower Moon. The Harvest Moon. All of them coincided with the Julian calendar. These women weren't witches. They had discovered the properties of the moon and its effects on nature just like any good scientist.

I turned to the final two pages of the book. On one side, a dark sky was littered with stars, reminding me of nights in Warrenville. A pale woman wore a dark cape, her hood pulled over her face. Only her arms were visible as they stretched toward the sky. She held an empty glass bowl in her hands.

"'The Dark Moon opens the doorway to different beliefs and an opportunity to change destiny. A doorway to new beginnings,'" I whispered.

The other side of the page was different. A full moon hung low in the sky, surrounded by clouds. A dark woman was in a red silk gown, her face hidden beneath long dark curls. She held a gilded harp in her arms like a shield.

The Full Moon must be treated with care, said the caption below her. *All caution should be taken during the Witching Hour, when the veil between the natural world and the spirit world disappears.*

It was then that I looked at the picture more closely. On first glance, stars littered the clouds that surrounded the moon. But after staring for another moment, I realized they weren't stars at all. They were eyes. Glowing haint eyes.

I was so fixated on the image that I didn't hear Janie call my name, and when she touched my arm, I yelped.

"What's wrong with you?" Janie frowned.

"You shouldn't sneak up on people like that." I put the book back on the shelf.

"Did you find anything?" she asked.

"Nothing that can tell us how to keep those haints from coming back to the house."

"It's been almost an hour. We should see if Mrs. Whitney can talk now."

I stood up and wiggled the cramps out of my legs. I was still thinking about the women. The Dark Moon. The Full Moon. The Witching Hour. Still no answers. If anything, I only had more questions.

CHAPTER SEVENTEEN

Amulets

Mrs. Whitney was standing in front of the display of the silver hands when we walked into the Train Depot. "You have a spiritual problem?" She didn't turn around to face us.

"Yes, ma'am," I said. Jasper must have told Mrs. Whitney that we needed an appointment. "We had some haints come to our house. We need to know what we can do to keep them from coming back."

Mrs. Whitney turned around. She was wearing another long white dress, and her hair tumbled around her shoulders. She wore the same collection of necklaces, and I stared at the large dark stone.

"Come with me." She passed the silver hands

display and turned down a short hallway to a room. We followed her inside.

It was a small, dank space lit by candles. A storage room with shelves of mason jars filled with spices and herbs overwhelmed my senses. Other jars were filled with things I didn't recognize, but I could have sworn I saw some chicken feet and snakeskins. I nervously rubbed my arms.

Everyone thought Mrs. Whitney was a witch, but I didn't see any pentagrams. No magic wands. Only a bowl of water and a stack of stones on a small card table. She motioned for us to sit in two metal folding chairs. The next few moments were filled with awkward silence before she sat down in front of us and stared.

Finally, I cleared my throat. "Do you think you can help us with our spiritual problem?"

"There has been a disturbance," Mrs. Whitney said as she lit three red candles. "I've had several appointments this week. *Something* has awakened the spirits in Warrenville. Do you girls know anything about this?"

I stole a glance at Janie. She was sitting straight in her chair, her mouth in a tight line. She wasn't going to confess anything.

"Is this about Creek Church?" I asked.

"Creek Church is just one place. The spirits have awakened all over town. I've had to deal with all kinds of mess. I wasn't quite ready yet, but it is what it is."

I swallowed hard. I thought Creek Church was the only haunted place. Hearing haints were coming out of the woodwork didn't comfort me at all.

"Do you know what did it? What woke them up?" Janie asked.

"No, but I have my theories," Mrs. Whitney said as she opened a jar of large seeds and placed them one by one in the water.

"Can you stop this?" I asked.

Mrs. Whitney didn't answer; she opened another mason jar filled with a pungent yellow powder. "The spirits were just outside the house? They didn't enter?" Mrs. Whitney poured the powder into the bowl.

"No, but they left handprints underneath my window," I said. "We think they were trying to find a way inside."

"That's good," Mrs. Whitney said. "Means they can't enter. Not yet."

Janie and I exchanged another look. I was glad that Ellis had decided to stay outside. He wouldn't like any of this. He'd probably have nightmares for months.

Mrs. Whitney opened another mason jar full of dried green leaves and crushed them in her hands before sprinkling them over the water. She took a wooden spoon and mixed everything together, then slowly started to hum a somber melody. I wondered if she was casting a spell. Janie gave Mrs. Whitney a rotten-egg stare.

"Are you making a potion?" I asked.

Mrs. Whitney ignored me and continued humming. On the table, she opened a straw basket and grabbed several strips of linen cloth. She poured the contents of the bowl through a filter and then placed a small amount of her concoction onto each strip, making little pouches with twine.

"I'm making amulets for your family," she said. "You should wear them on your person at all times."

"What's an amulet?" I asked.

"Protection," she replied.

I stared at the pouches on the table. I wouldn't be able to give Mama or Daddy a haint-protection pouch. I already knew that. There would be no way to explain why they needed them without getting into serious trouble.

"So you're gonna give us these pouches. That's it? How do we even know it works?" Janie crossed her arms, unimpressed.

"You can use whatever you like, child. Its power is in your belief." She touched the black stone necklace. I wondered if that was her amulet.

"What can we do to protect our house?" I asked.

"You can enforce a perimeter with iron or with blessed salt," Mrs. Whitney said.

"How does that do anything?" Janie asked.

"Patience, child. You came here for answers; I'm giving them to you." Mrs. Whitney met Janie's eyes and stared until Janie broke her gaze. "Iron rods or a horseshoe hung over a doorway can also prevent a spirit from entering. When salt is blessed, it acts as a holy protector. A spirit can't cross its path."

The room had quickly become hot and stuffy, and I squirmed in my chair. Mrs. Whitney was telling us what to do, but I didn't know if I believed her. Anything could protect us as long as we believed it could? That didn't make any sense. If anything could protect us, then why did she make us the pouches?

Mrs. Whitney blew out the candles, and the smoke floated across the table in lazy waves. "Is there anything else you want to tell me?"

Janie looked down at her hands and said nothing. *Mrs. Whitney didn't know we had gone to Creek Church or about the boy. I didn't want to be a snitch. I was afraid to tell Mrs. Whitney that we had woken the haints.*

"Why did you come back after all these years?" I asked.

"I came back to set the town's history right," Mrs. Whitney said.

She stood up and reached high on a shelf to grab a small wood statue. It was a handmade figure of a woman whittled by a sharp knife. She placed it on the table in front of us.

"Haints are trapped. This earthly plane is not their home anymore. They will always seek refuge until they are released to their true place of belonging. There is nothing to fear."

"What is that?" I pointed to the statue.

"This is an heirloom," she said. "A talisman that has been passed down in my family for generations. I'm going to let you hold her until we get this resolved. You can put her on your windowsill. She will watch over you."

I took the wooden statue off the table; it felt smooth and warm in my hand. "Thank you."

"What do we owe you for all of this?" Janie asked.

"I take all kinds of charity," Mrs. Whitney said.

Janie gave her a doubtful look. "You don't want any money?"

"Money is just one form of energy, child."

Janie took the pouches off the table and put them in her pink backpack. Mrs. Whitney guided us into the hallway, and I was happy to be out of the dark room. We left the gift shop and stepped into the steamy afternoon air.

Mrs. Whitney had told us what we needed to do to protect ourselves, but she didn't know the whole story. Were we the sole cause of the haints wandering around Warrenville or just a piece of the puzzle?

The bright sun tingled across my arms. Could we trust her? She may already have known. When I turned around to glance at the Train Depot, Mrs. Whitney was watching us from the gift shop window. When our eyes met, a nervous sensation bubbled through my stomach. Her expression was strange, as if she knew what I had been thinking.

CHAPTER EIGHTEEN
Salt and Sugar

Where are we gonna find blessed salt?" Janie asked. "That doesn't seem like something you can just buy at the store."

"We can get rock salt from Hawkins Hardware and can bless it ourselves," I said. "Ellis can say grace over it."

Janie frowned. "He's not a priest."

"Remember what Mrs. Whitney told us. You just have to have faith in your amulets. You have to believe." I touched the statue in my pocket.

We found Jasper and Ellis playing basketball in Marigold Park. They had started a pickup game with the Baxter Twins. Bonner and Bailey were smaller, and they circled Jasper and Ellis like two tiny titans.

Jasper was a star on the junior varsity team, but he fumbled with the ball, giving the little boys a chance to steal it away from him. When Bailey's chubby hands couldn't swat the ball fast enough, Bonner weaved in and made a defensive play, pushing Ellis onto the ground. He trotted down the court to the hoop for a layup. The twins yelled in victory.

Jasper beamed at them. "Great game! Y'all just too good for me."

Ellis grumbled as he got up, rubbing dust from his knees. "They play too rough."

Jasper walked over to us, a sheen of sweat on his forehead. "So what happened? How did the appointment go?"

We told them what Mrs. Whitney had given us for protection. Jasper nodded and pulled out a pouch from his shirt that he had tied on a long string.

"She made it for me this morning," he said. "I thought it was strange."

"Did you tell her about the boy you saw?" Ellis asked.

"It wasn't the right time," I said.

"What are you waiting for?" Ellis grumbled.

"It wasn't my place to tell her, but you should have. She needs to know," Jasper said.

"Maybe if we just take her advice with the amulets we'll be fine," Janie said.

"We're in this mess because of you," Ellis said. "In a few days, you'll be gone, and we'll still be here dealing with these haints."

"I took her to Creek Church," I said. "It's just as much my fault as hers."

Janie gave me a small smile. We didn't need to argue about this; we needed to be a team.

The four of us walked inside Hawkins Hardware and found a dusty bag of rock salt. Warrenville hadn't had a good snow in five years, and that only dusted the grass and roofs like spilled sugar. Mama had layered us up with coats, hats, and mittens. There wasn't enough for a snowman, but I remember making snow angels on the ground with Daddy and Ellis. Mama made us vanilla syrup slushes. By the end of the day, the snow had melted without a trace.

Mr. Hawkins was too busy watching baseball on the small TV behind the counter to pay us any mind, buying a bag of rock salt in the middle of the summer.

Outside the store, I held the bulky bag in my arms. "We're going to take this home, say grace over it, and then sprinkle it around the house."

"Can I get some gummy worms?" Ellis asked.

"We should go home and get this done," Janie said. "No one cares about your candy."

I knew it wasn't exactly my brother's sweet tooth but rather Sunnie Loren, the high school girl and only daughter of the Loren family, that made my brother want to buy candy. Even though I told him that his crush would never amount to anything, he wouldn't listen to me. He was hopeless. But I didn't need to share that with Janie.

Ellis took a longing look across the street at Loren's Grocery. I had to remember, after everything that had happened with Creek Church and the haints, he hadn't snitched on us not once.

"Let's just go in for a quick stop," I said. "Ellis, only one bag of gummy worms, okay?"

We walked across the street and entered Loren's Grocery. Daddy had told us that back in the day, during segregation, it was one of the only places we could shop. Even now, with all the fancy stores and specialty shops in Alton, most of the townsfolk still shopped at Loren's because it was a tradition woven into the fabric of Warrenville. The Loren family still owned it outright, and most of them took turns minding the store. I loved this place because it was like shopping at a dear family's home.

Ellis searched for his crush, but she wasn't at the counter. Only Mrs. Loren was there, cracking a roll of pennies to put in the cash register. He took a long sigh and tried to hide his disappointment as he walked down the aisle to get his candy.

"Hey, y'all. Come to buy some sugar?" Mrs. Loren laughed.

"Yes, ma'am," I said.

We followed Ellis down the candy aisle. He had grabbed a bag of sour gummy worms and a king-size chocolate bar. I watched Janie closely as she moved farther down to the potato chips. Jasper stood in front of the gum rack and rubbed his chin, deep in decision making.

"You can't have both," I told Ellis. "You have to choose."

"I got money," he protested. "I can buy my own stuff."

"You remember what Mama said about cavities?" I reminded him.

"Fine." He put the candy bar back on the shelf. "The gummy worms will last longer anyway."

I turned when I heard Mrs. Loren greet another customer and groaned. A woman in a yellow dress with matching heels stood in front of the cash register.

"Mrs. Greene, I must say you look like new money. Aging like fine wine."

"Thank you, Sharla. I'm on my way to the church, but I wanted to stop by and see if Old Thomas had brought anything up from his land."

I crouched down in the aisle and motioned for the others to do so as well. Maybe if we were lucky, we wouldn't be seen, but I already knew that wouldn't be possible.

"No, he ain't been in today. He's running late. He brought some tomatoes yesterday if you want to go look but no meat. You know his daddy has been under the weather." Mrs. Loren continued, "But your grandbabies are in here."

"Why she gotta mention us?" Ellis mumbled. "She can't hold water in a tank."

"Just act normal," I said. "It'll be fine."

Mrs. Greene came down the aisle, and we all stood a little straighter. She narrowed her eyes at us as she did her inspections.

"Ellis, what have you been doing?" She frowned. "Why do your knees look like you been kicking flour in a field of mud?"

"I've been playing basketball with Jasper," he said.

Mrs. Greene took two of Janie's braids, rubbing

them between her fingers. "We need to find you a hair scarf before this frizz gets out of hand."

Then our grandma turned to me. "Does your mama know you're out here gallivanting in the streets?"

"I told Mrs. Taylor we were coming to Town Square," I said. "We were just on our way back home."

She studied the bag in my arms. "Why in the Lord's name do you have rock salt?"

Jasper took it from me. "I need it for my birdbaths."

Mrs. Greene squinted at him, and he took two steps backward, fear and uncertainty in his eyes.

"Young man, this bag is yours, but you've got my granddaughter holding it for you? What kind of home training have you had?"

"Sorry, ma'am," Jasper said.

"Will we see you later at the house?" I asked hopefully.

"I don't think so," she said. "You're coming with me. I need to keep an eye on you."

Ellis and Janie frowned but didn't say anything. They knew better. I turned to Jasper. "Good luck cleaning your birdbaths."

Jasper looked confused for a second but then got the hint: *Hold on to our rock salt until later.* "Right."

He walked to the front of the store and then turned to give us one last look of pity before he left.

Mrs. Greene took the bag of gummy worms out of my brother's hands and put it back on the shelf. She poked his tummy. "You need to stop eating this mess. Let's go."

"Have a blessed day!" Mrs. Greene smiled at Mrs. Loren as she guided us out of the store. After she let the door close, she shook her head. "Someone needs to go in there and mop those floors. Such a disgrace."

So much for summer freedom.

CHAPTER NINETEEN
The Deaconess

Mrs. Greene drove up the hill to the Missionary Creek Baptist Church. When I was a little girl, the church was like a home away from home; this was where Mrs. Greene spent most of her time. She was a deaconess, which meant she held a very prominent role. But not as important as the pastor's wife, who was the first lady of the church. Still, it seemed everyone deferred to my grandma when decisions needed to be made. Granddaddy Greene had been a deacon and a proud son of Warrenville; he returned after going to Morehouse College in Atlanta. He was one of the few. Daddy said one of the reasons he came back was to pay it forward to the community that helped raise him.

We walked into the foyer of the church, and Ellis grabbed a handful of mints and stashed them in his pocket before Mrs. Greene could catch him. I stood beside Janie as she read the church community bulletin board.

Mary Jenkins had posted about her lost pet. No one had the heart to tell her the cat had gone feral and was living in the woods behind her house. Teeter Collins was still looking for someone to buy his neon-green Cadillac. Jolinda Bell announced she had started a catering service, even though she had been banned from bringing potato salad to any further church functions.

We followed Mrs. Greene into the sanctuary, where the other members of the Deaconess Board were waiting.

"Can we go downstairs?" Ellis knew there were comics and games in the children's choir room.

"No," Mrs. Greene said. "You're gonna sit in the back while I attend this meeting. I want to be able to see you."

The women of the Deaconess Board sat in the front pews: Mrs. Jackson lived on our block and brought us peaches from her family's orchard, Mrs. Collins was a retired Fairfield County court clerk who knew Mama, and Mrs. Hudson was a retired teacher who had taught Daddy when he was in elementary school. Everyone had a connection to one another. They were all women with light skin and loose wavy hair. They could have passed for Mrs. Greene's sisters. So different from Mrs. Whitney with her dark skin and textured hair.

I wondered if it was Mrs. Greene who had broken off the friendship. I thought of Jovita at the Alton Mall with the Jones Girls. Did my grandma drop Mrs. Whitney for these women? The questions made my stomach clench in anxious waves.

"I'm sorry I'm late," Mrs. Greene said. "I had to fetch my grandchildren. Found them running around Town Square."

The women greeted us with hugs. There was always something comforting about getting smushed by a deaconess. Janie displayed her rotten-egg face after each woman squeezed her. She wasn't used to the Warrenville tradition of invading personal spaces.

"Now y'all go sit down and be quiet," Mrs. Greene said.

Janie and Ellis followed me as we went down several pews and sat toward the back. Janie pulled out her phone, and Ellis took sneaky gobbles of the church mints he had stashed away.

After the Deaconess Board said a small devotional prayer, Mrs. Hudson put on her glasses and pulled out a notebook. "We need to hammer out the details on this clothing drive."

"The main donations we need are for men's clothes," Mrs. Jackson added.

"Lena, you should think about giving away some of William's clothes to a deserving gentleman," Mrs. Collins said. "It's been two years now since he passed."

My grandma gave Mrs. Collins a dagger stare. "My husband's clothes are not up for donation. I don't need some diminished man wearing his clothes."

"Have you at least moved the clothes out of your bedroom?" Mrs. Hudson asked. "It's not healthy, Lena. You're taking this widow thing too far."

Mrs. Greene's face fell for a moment. It was just a flicker of emotion, but I had seen it. And just as quick as it surfaced, so did her pursed lips, straightened posture, and lifted chin. "Do I look like a widow to you?" she asked with a smirk.

After about an hour, my eyelids grew heavy, but at least I was still upright. Ellis had fallen to the side, his eyes closed and his mouth wide open, low snores escaping through his lips. Janie had slumped over as well.

I was about to give up and make a pallet of the church pew for an epic nap when something sparked my attention.

"So the festival board has officially denied Denise Whitney's booth?" Mrs. Hudson asked. "I don't know what that woman was thinking, trying to bring that mess to Marigold Park."

"The dead should be left alone. They are in the arms of Jesus," Mrs. Collins added.

"Amen," Mrs. Greene said.

"Well, tricksters are among us. They always try to lead us astray," Mrs. Jackson offered.

"The devil is a liar," Mrs. Greene said. "We know the truth. God is good."

"All the time," the women answered in unison.

I frowned. If what Mrs. Whitney said was true, Warrenville had a lot of spiritual problems to solve. We had seen it firsthand. The haints needed to be released by their blood kin. Maybe this is what Mrs. Whitney wanted to achieve with the booth. Many townsfolk treated the Heritage Festival as a homecoming to reconnect with family. Perhaps this was the opportunity she needed for all of the town's blood kin to come together and release the spirits once and for all.

"I'm still mad she had the money to buy the Train Depot in the first place," Mrs. Hudson complained. "We could have done so much with that location."

"Have you been in her gift shop?" Mrs. Jackson asked.

"Wouldn't be caught dead in that place." Mrs. Greene shook her head in dismay.

"I've heard she's practicing rootwork in the back room," Mrs. Jackson whispered.

"Lord Jesus." Mrs. Collins picked up an MLK fan and waved away the scandal of it.

"That's not what she's doing," I called out.

It wasn't until the words had escaped that I realized I had opened my mouth. The women looked at me. Mrs. Greene's mouth was set in her trademark frown.

"How do you know what she's doing or not doing?" Mrs. Greene said. "Why are you listening to grown folks business?"

I stood up from the pew. Janie stirred and woke up, rubbing her eyes.

"I don't think it's fair to make assumptions about Mrs. Whitney. At least not without hard evidence," I said. "What you're stating is a hypothesis. You have to prove your theory through observation."

The other women looked at Mrs. Greene. Her cheeks were flushed pink. I had embarrassed her in front of the Deaconess Board.

"I think the heat has gotten to this child." Mrs. Greene stood up and smoothed out her dress. "Let's adjourn this meeting so I can take my grandchildren home."

Janie shoved Ellis awake, and he jerked up, wiping slobber from his cheek. "What I miss?"

Mrs. Greene came down the aisle, latched on to my elbow, and dragged me out of the pew. "Don't you ever sass me in front of my board again," she hissed in my ear between clenched teeth.

My heart beat fast in my chest. Janie looked at me, concerned. Ellis was utterly confused. Mrs. Greene remained silent for the rest of the ride home.

CHAPTER TWENTY
Family Meeting

By the time Mrs. Greene finished the rest of her errands in Alton and she pulled into our driveway, Mama was already home. She met us in the kitchen and smiled broadly when she saw Mrs. Greene, which was odd. Mama was never this happy to see our grandma.

"Lena, I appreciate you calling me about the children. We would love you to stay for supper."

"Is that right, Delilah?" Mrs. Greene pushed her heavy purse into my arms. *What did she put in here?* Ellis used to joke that it was probably the severed head of an enemy.

"Robert would like to have a family meeting," Mama said. "He wanted to be sure you were included."

Mrs. Greene inspected the kitchen as Mama spoke. She frowned before walking over to touch the stove. "Too cold for supper."

Mama ignored her and took off her jacket. "Your son is bringing the food. He's on his way. You can rest while we wait. Would you like some sweet tea?"

"Ice water will do."

Mama gave her a tall glass, and Mrs. Greene left the kitchen and went into the living room. Janie followed her, while Ellis made gagging faces behind our grandma's back.

I stayed in the kitchen with Mama as she opened her briefcase and shuffled out some of her law office papers.

"What's this family meeting about?" I asked.

Mama didn't seem upset, so it probably wasn't about Creek Church. I wondered if there would be a time when I needed to tell her everything, or if Mrs. Whitney would beat me to it. I hoped not.

Mama smiled and brushed my cheek. "We have a slight change in plans for the summer."

"Did something bad happen?" I asked.

"Everything is fine, Sarah."

Mama headed upstairs, leaving me more confused than ever. A change in plans? My mind rattled with the different possible meanings for this.

Daddy came home with three boxes of pizza. Ellis beamed. Mrs. Greene was not impressed.

"Does anyone cook anymore around here?" she complained.

I grabbed the paper plates from the cupboard, and we all went into the dining room. Mrs. Greene looked around her chair and under the table. I'm sure she thought Walter would come leaping into her lap like last time.

"Don't worry," Daddy reassured her. "Ellis learned his lesson."

Ellis smiled at Mrs. Greene; she only narrowed her eyes at him. "Humph. You still need the wrath of a good switch."

Our grandma took a napkin and pressed down on her slice until it was transparent with grease. Then she cut her cheese pizza as if she was dining at the finest steak restaurant, eating filet mignon.

Mama and Daddy still hadn't mentioned what the family meeting was about. I tried to enjoy my pizza, but it felt like cardboard on my tongue. Janie took small bites of her pepperoni slice in silence.

Ellis was on his third slice when Daddy finally

cleared his throat, the signal he was beginning the family meeting.

"So the reason I called us together is to share some news with all of you."

Mrs. Greene put down her knife. "Are you starting your own business?"

"This isn't about me," Daddy said. "Gina called me a few hours ago, and there's been a change in plans."

Ellis and I glanced at each other. He looked just as confused as I was. Janie sat straight up in her chair. "What does that mean?"

"Gina's screen test went exceptionally well," Mama said.

Mrs. Greene released a short snort but remained silent.

"That's right," Daddy said. "Janie, your mama is gonna be in a movie!"

Janie jumped up and screamed, the sound making me whip my palms to my ears.

"My mom is gonna be a movie star?!"

"You need to control your volume, young lady," Mrs. Greene warned.

Janie stopped yelling.

"Not yet, but she's been cast in a movie." Mama

reached across the table and squeezed Janie's hand. "A supporting role. A good one. Which means she'll have to go film on location in Paris—"

Mama couldn't even finish her sentence because Janie started whooping and hollering.

"Can you use your indoor scream, please?" Ellis complained.

"Paris?! Oh my God, oh my God," Janie chanted.

Mrs. Greene dabbed the corner of her mouth. "Gina can't stay off a plane."

"When do I leave?" Janie squealed. "How soon can I go?"

Mama and Daddy exchanged heavy looks. It was then that I knew what Mama had meant in the kitchen. The change in summer plans. Janie wouldn't be going to Paris at all.

"Your mother will be very busy," Mama explained. "She won't have any time to spend with you, and she needs to prepare for her role."

Janie's smile vanished. "But she told me that if she became a movie star, she would come get me. She promised."

"I know this is hard," Daddy said.

"So does this mean the girl is staying in Warrenville?" Mrs. Greene asked.

"Yes, for the rest of the summer," Mama said. "We thought it would be best for everyone."

Janie slumped in her chair. The rotten-egg grimace plain on her face. "I hate it here."

"Honey, I thought you were having a good time?" Mama asked softly.

"She promised me," Janie said quietly.

"Maybe now is a good time for us to have a different kind of talk," Mrs. Greene stated. "I found these children up in Loren's Grocery, unsupervised."

Mama looked at Mrs. Greene. "I've told Sarah she could go to Town Square as long as Mrs. Taylor knows where she is."

"That's another thing," Mrs. Greene continued. "It doesn't make any sense that a woman who is not our blood kin is looking after these children."

Mama took a deep breath. "Lena, for the hundredth time, these are my children. Not yours."

"Janie isn't your child," Mrs. Greene spat back. "She's my granddaughter. She needs to be somewhere where she can be supervised."

"Everyone here is being taken care of," Mama said.

"How would you know? You're not even here!" Mrs. Greene shouted.

The room went silent. Ellis slid down in his chair. Janie was fighting back tears. I was too scared to move.

"Sarah, Ellis, why don't you two go upstairs," Daddy said more as a command than a question. "I think we need to have a private conversation with Janie and your grandma."

Ellis shot up from the table. "Can I take a slice of pizza with me?"

"No," my parents replied in unison.

"I'm still hungry, though," Ellis mumbled.

I took my brother's hand, and we left the dining room. Janie had been right about her mama. Aunt Gina was on her way to being a movie star, and she would finally be a celebrity daughter.

This also meant that my cousin was under my watch for the rest of the summer.

CHAPTER TWENTY-ONE

Daphnis

Since the start of her stay, Janie had collected pens, stamps, even stickers from bananas. I stared at the wall above her bed, where she had taped pictures from her celebrity magazines. I stared at palm trees and famous movie stars. She had brought California to Warrenville. Just like I loved my planets and moons, Janie loved her beaches and mansions. She'd made the other side of my room her home.

I continued to stare at Janie's wall until my eyes blurred. Although I loved science and space, I didn't think I could live in a world alone with them. I couldn't imagine being anywhere without my family. Although Janie had collected wonderful and unusual things, she was still all by herself. Her mama had made a promise, and now that promise had been broken.

I reached in my pocket and touched the wood statue from Mrs. Whitney. I had almost forgotten about it. I pulled it out and looked at its smooth surface. My fingers traveled down the woman's arms. She reminded me of a warrior. I decided to name the statue Daphnis. It was a new moon discovered by the Cassini spacecraft. It had the same qualities of the wooden statue. An irregular shape and a smooth surface. I smiled at Daphnis as I put her on the windowsill.

Mama's voice floated up the stairs. She was using her lawyer voice with Mrs. Greene. Their words were sharp and traveled to my room in loud, angry waves. I froze as they reached a furious crescendo and the front door slammed shut, abruptly cutting them off.

A few moments later Janie appeared in the doorway. Her face was hard to read. I couldn't tell if she was happy or if she was sad.

My cousin didn't say anything to me. Instead she crawled on top of the bed and started to peel her poster collage off the wall.

"What are you doing?" I crossed the room and

stared at the pictures discarded around her feet like trash.

My brother poked his head in. "Did y'all hear all that yelling?"

"Not now, Ellis."

Janie continued to scrape posters filled with pictures of movie stars and mansions off the wall. When the tape held fast, she ripped them away. Ellis and I glanced at each other. We had never seen Janie damage any of her things before.

"Did you find out what kind of movie your mama's gonna be in?" Ellis asked. "Is Aunt Gina gonna be in something like that movie *Alien*? Maybe she can get one of those slimy things to bust out of her belly."

"I don't care." She fell onto her pillow and let out a sigh.

"Why was Mrs. Greene hollering like some crazy woman downstairs?" Ellis continued.

"She wanted me to stay with her in that old-lady house."

I glimpsed at Ellis, who shrugged. "We don't mind if you stay with us," I reassured her.

The fact that Janie was staying should have bothered me, but it didn't anymore. All I had craved was peace and quiet. My plans revolved around reading my Cassini book and learning everything about Saturn's moons. Now things were different. I had gotten used to Janie being in my room. It made me forget how lonely I was without Jovita.

"Living with two girls ain't been too bad," Ellis added. "Now you can help out with the haints."

We heard a quick knock, and Mama came into the room. She had changed into her silk floral robe and had pulled her hair up in a messy bun. A faint crease appeared between her brows.

"What are you doing out of your room?" she asked Ellis.

Ellis stumbled and tripped over Janie's fuzzy slippers. "I was checking to see if Janie was all right."

Ellis quickly left, and Mama closed the door. She stared at the bare wall, then lowered her gaze to the torn posters on Janie's bed.

My cousin crossed her arms. "I didn't want anything that reminds me of California."

Mama examined Janie's face for a moment. "You might change your mind later."

"Is Mrs. Greene mad at you? Why was she yelling like that?" I asked.

Mama rubbed the back of her neck. "Your grandmother and I have a difference of opinion on where

Janie should stay this summer. She'll be fine."

"If it makes any difference, Ellis and I decided Janie should stay here too."

Mama's face relaxed, and she pressed her lips into a smile. The knots loosened in my stomach, and I took in a deep breath. "We're family," she said as she kissed both of us on our foreheads. "Our home is Janie's home too."

Janie slid off the bed and pulled her nightgown out of the dresser.

"You don't mind that I'm staying?" Janie asked. "You're not lying, are you?"

It wasn't her fault that she couldn't go to Paris with her mama, and we couldn't let Janie stay at Mrs. Greene's house. I didn't hate her that much. I wasn't even sure I hated her at all.

"Of course not," I said. "I wouldn't wish staying at Mrs. Greene's house on my worst enemy."

"Not even those country birds we saw at the mall?" Janie asked.

"Maybe Mrs. Greene could give them some home training. Teach those Jones Girls how to act." I smiled.

"This whole night has made my head hurt," Janie said. "I'm going to take my bath."

. . .

I ventured down the hall to my parents' bedroom. Mama sat at her dressing table. She slid creamy lotion on her legs, and I watched it disappear into her skin.

I stood behind her chair, staring at Mama in her vanity mirror.

"Are you okay, Sarah?" she asked.

"Why can't Janie stay with her daddy in Chicago?"

She gestured for me to come closer. When she squeezed me into a hug, I could smell the citrus scent on her skin. "I thought you said that it was fine if she stayed here for the summer."

"I did." I paused. "But I don't think she's happy about it."

"You know the situation with Janie's father. He's remarried now." She rubbed her hand against my cheek. "Things are complicated."

"She never talks about him," I said. "She barely talks to me at all."

Mama sighed. "Give her some time. Some people deal with hard things in different ways."

I thought about this for a moment. Until now I had only focused on my own problems. I hadn't thought about what Janie might be going through. I was so wrapped up in keeping her out of trouble.

Invested in trying to protect us against the haints.

"I need you to try harder," Mama said. "Janie needs to know that she's a part of this family. I know you're used to having things done your way, but I need your help in this. Do you think you can do that for me?"

"I'll try," I said.

"Good." She picked up her brush from the dressing table. "You want to practice your braiding on me?"

"I don't need practice anymore," I said.

"Even better. Let's see what you can do," she said. "Go get my coconut oil."

When I returned from the bathroom, Mama was on the carpet. I sat in the chair, and she nestled between my knees. I parted her hair into sections and layered coconut oil on her scalp. After giving her a good head massage, I brushed her hair in long, deep strokes. I decided to give her a big goddess braid.

She stood up and admired my work in the vanity mirror. "Very nice."

"Thanks," I said, a huge smile spreading across my face.

CHAPTER TWENTY-TWO

Protect This House

The next morning, I woke up and inspected my bedroom window and the backyard. Daphnis was standing undisturbed on the sill, a silent sentry of protection. I touched the glass pane and took a deep sigh of relief.

Janie was still burrowed in her sheets.

I knew my cousin didn't want to be in Warrenville, but now that she was here for the summer, we needed to figure out how to fix the mess we had created. Maybe she would come in handy in getting rid of the haints. And just maybe we'd figure out how to be better friends.

At breakfast, my parents poked around with questions to make sure everything was okay. Mama once again declared her confidence in me to take care of everything while she was at work. It made me wince because I hadn't been taking care of things. My parents' protection pouches were still in Janie's backpack. When they left, we could at least protect the house. We had been lucky that nothing had come to visit in the dead of night, but I didn't want to take any chances.

Later that morning, Jasper came over on his bike with the rock salt. He carried it in a large black trash bag and lugged it over his shoulder as he climbed up the porch steps.

"Where's Janie and Ellis?" he asked.

"Ellis is upstairs brushing his teeth," I replied. "Janie is still in bed."

Jasper looked at his watch.

"She usually sleeps late, but I also think it's because she's sad. Her mama got a role in a movie in Paris, and she has to stay here."

"That's kind of messed up," Jasper said.

We sat down on the top porch step. "Ready to put this salt down?" he asked, changing the subject.

"I hope it works. A summer storm can wash everything away. Maybe it's more the ceremony of it?"

"Maybe." He paused. "Do you think the haints we saw at Creek Church can be saved?"

"I don't know," I said. "Now having woken them up, I'm not sure yet if that's good or bad."

"Mrs. Whitney wants to save them," Jasper said.

"What happened at Creek Church wasn't right."

"No it wasn't," he agreed.

"They never got any kind of justice," I added, the angry heat rising up through my arms and my chest until my face burned. "No one talks about it anymore. The more I think about it, the more it makes me angry."

"You should be angry," Jasper said. "Mrs. Whitney says we can't change the past, but we need to remember it. We need to acknowledge it and not hide it."

I thought about my own memories. All I knew was Mama, Daddy, Ellis, and Mrs. Greene. I didn't have perfect memories. I didn't have a perfect family. Not with my grandma's inspections and constant judgments. When I thought of Warrenville's history . . . *those* memories were acts of pure evil. They were haunting, most of them too painful to bring up. Maybe this is why Mrs. Greene never talked about her childhood.

Ellis came out on the porch and plopped down next to us. "You bring the salt?"

"Yep," Jasper said.

"Let's get started," Ellis said. "The sooner I can protect myself from a haint the better."

I stood up. The boys went down the porch steps, but I didn't follow them. "Let me go get Janie," I said.

"We'll start looking around the house to get our perimeter set up," Jasper called out as they walked away. "Meet us in the backyard."

I went inside and headed up the stairs. When I opened the door to my bedroom, Janie was still underneath the covers.

"Janie?" I whispered.

When she didn't answer me, I touched her shoulder.

"Leave me alone," she mumbled.

"Jasper is downstairs with the salt," I said. "We're going to bless it and put it around the house. Maybe those haint things will leave us alone then."

She moaned and shifted away from me. "I don't care about the stupid salt."

"Janie, this is important," I said. "We can't let the haints get inside the house."

My cousin didn't budge. She moved closer to the

wall. I wasn't sure what else to say. What do you tell someone who is missing their mama? I had never been away from my own mama for more than a few days. How would I feel if I knew I wouldn't see her smile or be able to brush her hair and give her a goddess braid? If I couldn't share a bagel with her in the morning? I didn't know how any of that felt, but I knew that it had to hurt. That heavy feeling at the bottom of your stomach. The sharp sting of tears that never come. I knew what it felt like to miss a best friend.

I tugged at her blanket again. "Janie, I know you feel bad. I don't know if there's anything I can do to make you feel better. It's not fair that you can't go to Paris and be with your mama. You should be with her and not with us. But since you're with us, I want you to know that I'm here for you. And we want you to help us."

Janie peeked out from underneath the covers. Her eyes were red, as if she had been crying.

"I know she promised you," I continued. "But I'm sure she meant California and not Paris! I mean, do you even have a passport? By the time you got one, she would be done with the movie. Think of all the fancy things she'll get you. Authentic French stuff. I'm kind of jealous."

Janie sat up in the bed and took off her hair scarf, rubbing the satin with her fingers. "I really miss her."

"Of course you do—I would miss my mama too," I said. "But she left you here because she knew you were safe and with family. People who care about you. I don't think she would be happy to know you're sad."

Janie fiddled with the scarf, winding it around her hands. "I'm sorry I haven't been that nice to you."

"That's okay. I'm sorry for being a bossy nag." I smiled, remembering what she had called me that day at Mrs. Greene's house.

Janie smiled back at me. "You're really good at that."

"Whatever," I said, getting up from her bed. "Get dressed and come downstairs. We have work to do!"

Jasper had fetched two ceramic angels from Mama's garden.

"Figured we could put the angels on the front porch," Jasper said.

I touched one of the wings. "Easy enough to put faith in angels," I said.

Ellis had gathered up horseshoes that Granddaddy Duncan had left on his last visit. I still remember the clangs and ringing of the game they played during Mama's birthday celebration.

"We can put these near the back door," I said.

Janie came out into the backyard, her braids pulled up in a high ponytail. Her eyes were less red now, and she went over and took some of the horseshoes from Ellis.

After placing the angels on the front porch and the horseshoes near the back door, I worried Mama would think something was going on, but maybe she wouldn't notice.

We gathered around the rock salt, and I opened up the bag, releasing a puff of white smoke that caused me to cough.

"So we're gonna say a short grace over this and then sprinkle it around the house. Especially near the woods," I said. "Ellis, are you ready?"

"I still don't feel like we're leaving this blessing in the best hands," Janie said. "We need a professional. A real priest."

"I got this," Ellis said.

"You have to be serious," I told him. "No fooling around."

"Sarah, I know. I got this." Ellis bowed his head, and the rest of us did the same.

"Dear Lord, bless this salt as we use it to protect against restless spirits. Let this salt hold the haints at bay and keep our family safe. Let this salt protect us as we sleep. Let this salt protect us against any evil that may dwell in the night. Let this salt protect us from bodily harm. In your name, we pray. Amen."

"That was a nice prayer," Jasper said.

Ellis smiled and gave everyone two handfuls of salt out of the bag.

I hoped it was enough.

CHAPTER TWENTY-THREE
Fireworks

My brother's prayer over the salt must have been strong and true, because we endured another haint-free night.

The next day was the Fourth of July, and the fireworks were a Fairfield County tradition. Everyone came out to see them. I remember last year, lying on the grass and staring up at the sky with Jovita, waiting for dusk to turn to nightfall. Waiting to see colors explode in the sky and rain down to the earth like shooting stars. I found out later on that different elements determined the colors of fireworks. Lithium carbonate made red. Sodium nitrate made yellow. Barium chloride made green. I imagined the fireworks as nebulas forming new suns, birthplaces for planets and moons.

Daddy snaked through the traffic at Fairfield Park and backed into a tight corner of the packed parking lot. We grabbed the folding chairs, and Mama pulled out a large cooler.

Earlier that day we had had a cookout in the backyard. Daddy put hamburgers and hot dogs on his green-domed grill. Mama put ears of corn and made veggie kabobs from Mrs. Greene's garden. Our grandma didn't make an appearance. She insisted she had been invited to Pastor Munroe's house, but I wondered if that just meant she was still mad at Mama for letting Janie stay with us.

Ellis had eaten too many hot dogs, so he stayed closed to Mama, resting his head in her lap. Although Janie teased him, his stomach must have ached more than his pride, because he ignored her.

I spread out a blanket on the grass. The sky was turning a deep indigo, and the fireflies were making an appearance with their iridescent green flashes.

Janie sprawled across the blanket, and I lay down next to her, our heads touching. She released a long sigh.

"Mom takes me to the Navy Pier to see the fireworks," Janie said. "This is different."

"Jovita hates the loud booms," I said. "She always covers her ears."

Saying her name out loud made my heart skip. Jovita had always come with us to Fairfield Park to watch the fireworks since her mama usually worked that day. She didn't like them, but she came because I loved them and she was my best friend.

Now I didn't know if she was here at Fairfield Park, lying on a blanket with the Jones Girls. I wouldn't know if she capped her ears with the palms of her hands to push out the noise.

"Is Jovita your only friend?" Janie asked.

I paused. Jovita had been my best friend, but was she my only friend? I furrowed my brow. Amber Cassidy chatted with me in class but sometimes acted like she didn't see me in the hallways when she was with her other friends. Carmen Simmons sat next to me in gym class, whining about push-ups, but when we left the locker room, we didn't have too much to say to each other.

Jovita had been the only girl who talked to me outside of school, the only one who invited me to hang out with her on weekends. She listened to my obsession with astronomy even though she didn't understand most of what I was saying.

I thought about Amber and Carmen. Amber with her pale skin and eyes the color of the ocean. Carmen with her freckles and curly hair. Neither one had ever been to my house. They never contacted me over the summer. Should I have more friends? Maybe there was something wrong with me?

"I know some other girls from school," I said. "But they're not really my friends."

"Girls are the worst," Janie said.

"What about you? Do you have any friends? You never talk about anyone else from Chicago."

Janie sighed and moved closer to me. "Mom is my best friend."

"That's not the same," I said. "Your mama is always gonna like you, until you break a rule, and then she'll just be disappointed."

"Girls at my school don't like me," Janie replied.

"Girls at my school bully me for no good reason," I added.

Janie turned on her side to face me. "Oh, they have a reason. You're smart. You make them feel dumb, which they probably are anyway. They know you're gonna be someone important one day, while they'll just be regular people."

"Maybe," I said, not quite believing her.

"It's true," she said. "You're the smartest girl I know."

I grabbed her hand and squeezed it.

"People tell me that I'm a show-off. A know-it-all," I confessed. "But I just like facts. And I like asking questions."

"You do like asking questions!" Janie laughed.

"Why don't the girls like you at your school?"

Janie shifted again and stared up at the dark sky. "When my dad left, I lost my friends. We had to move into a smaller apartment, and some of them said they couldn't visit me on the bad side of town."

"Those weren't your real friends," I said.

"Exactly," Janie said. "When Mom gets movie-star famous and I become a celebrity daughter, they'll come back running, and I'm going to ignore them. I hate fake people."

"Me too," I said. "I just want a real friend."

"Yeah." Janie squeezed my hand. "In the meantime, we'll have each other's backs."

The first firework shot up like a tiny rocket going

into space and burst open into a rosebud of sparkle. The boom reverberated in my heart. I lay there in the grass, watching the sky explode in color. In this moment everything felt right. I wasn't scared, and I wasn't sad. As I lay on the grass, watching fireworks with my family, nothing else mattered.

CHAPTER TWENTY-FOUR
A Past Life

Over the next week, Janie got over her sad phase. She went back to daily pedicures, and I went back to studying the Cassini spacecraft mission and Saturn's moons while everyone slept in. It hadn't rained yet, so our blessed salt still protected us from night visits from the haints. At least this is what I wanted to believe. To avoid questions from Mama, we kept our amulets hidden in our pockets. Mrs. Whitney said we just needed to have faith, and every morning I bolstered my belief as I kissed Daphnis on her wooden head, thankful for her extra protection.

Janie and I did more things together. Her taste for troublemaking and snooping didn't seem to be as important anymore. I lured her away from Mrs.

Taylor's reality TV and convinced her to watch the *History of the Solar System* series with me. Even though I had already watched all of the episodes, I enjoyed it more the second time around and took copious notes. I couldn't wait to go the science symposium in September.

Ellis let us alone in our girl cocoon, and I found that I no longer cared that Jovita wasn't my best friend anymore. She hadn't called me. She still hadn't invited me to her birthday party, but it didn't matter as much. The heavy gloom I felt in my chest finally went away.

On Saturday morning after breakfast, Jasper came over on his bike to meet up with Ellis so Daddy could take them to a basketball day camp. Mama decided to bury the hatchet with Mrs. Greene and drove us over to her house so we could help our grandma sort out some of Granddaddy Greene's belongings for the church clothing drive. I guess she had taken to heart what the women had told her at the Deaconess Board meeting. It was time for her to let go of things from the past.

Mama sat on the couch in the parlor, and Mrs. Greene gave her a glass of sweet tea. Janie and I stood and waited. Since our grandma didn't offer us anything to drink, it was a signal that they were about to discuss grown folks business without us.

Mrs. Greene gave us several large plastic bags and told us to go into the attic and find suitable things for the clothing drive.

The sun was directly over the house and warmed the attic with its oppressive heat. The lone window gave everything a dim glow as I surveyed old furniture covered with dusty white sheets, broken toys spilling from boxes, and large leather trunks with thick films of dust bunnies.

"Still junky as ever," Janie said.

Our grandma was immaculate in all other parts of her house, but apparently the attic didn't count; it was haphazard and full of chaos. It was a room hidden from guests and judgmental inspections. I sneezed from the stale air and dust.

"We have to be careful. In case something falls on us," I said.

Looking through the boxes, I found several of Granddaddy's ties, shirts, and suspenders. Granddaddy Greene had always dressed in a suit and wore a hat. The official uniform of a mortician. I remembered the smell of his hugs, a mix of tobacco and mint.

During his last days in hospice, I had gone with Daddy to sit by his bedside. I remembered Daddy reading aloud *Invisible Man*, which was one of Granddaddy Greene's favorite novels.

"Do you think he can hear you?" I had asked.

"Yes, I believe he can," Daddy had told me. "I have to believe he can hear his son."

Wrapping a tie around my wrist, I deeply inhaled Granddaddy Greene's familiar scent. I thought maybe this was the real reason that Mrs. Greene had sent us up here to the attic. Maybe she didn't want to relive these memories. Maybe it was still too soon.

I had filled two bags of clothes when Janie called me over to her corner of the attic. She had opened up a big leather trunk. I noticed a lock on the floor next to her feet.

"How did you get the trunk open?" I asked.

She blinked her eyes. "It fell open."

When I frowned at her, she sighed. "It didn't take much for me to jiggle it open. It was an old lock, and I was curious. Take a look at all this stuff."

"These are private things," I protested.

Janie plunged into the contents, pulling out papers. "I'm tired of looking at old-people clothes. This is way more interesting."

Despite my reluctance, I peered inside. The worn leather had deep scrapes. This was the kind of trunk that had traveled many long journeys across lands and oceans. A treasure chest of many lifetimes.

Janie scavenged through and uncovered jewelry tinged with opal and nickel. None of it was real, but it still seemed priceless. Janie tried on several bracelets and rings. There was a folded dress of white cotton and crocheted lace. Pictures of women in high-neck dresses and feather-plume hats. Faded baby pictures with moth-eaten edges. We found several Bibles, birth certificates, and school diplomas. There were also many leather-bound books. I picked up one and opened it. The first page was filled with small, frilly cursive.

November 12, 1947

Miss Hamilton gave me this diary as a gift for my birthday because I have done well with my lessons. She said that I could use it to write down my thoughts. I have so many thoughts. So many that I think they may burst from my head and float into the sky for all the world to see.

I wept when I heard the news. Our beloved church burned to the ground. We cannot even have a safe sanctuary. They took our place of worship. We praise the same God, yet we are not seen as human. This is the lie they tell themselves, but we know the truth. We are flesh and bone. We hurt and we bleed. This is one thing they will acknowledge. Our blood. They know our blood well. They ache to see it spill and seep into the ground. But even our blood is worthless to them. No justice for the terror they inflict on us. Miss Hamilton says God is on our side, and He will help us rebuild the church. I want to believe, but I'm losing my faith.

I studied the handwriting. Blots of smeared dried ink and mildew filled in the crevice of the yellowed pages. The pit of my stomach fluttered with curiosity.

"Look at this, Janie." I offered the book to her. "This could be a girl's diary by the handwriting."

My cousin took it and read quickly. "You think this belonged to Mrs. Greene?"

"No, it was written in 1947," I said. "I don't think Mrs. Greene was even alive then."

Janie flipped through the rest of the pages, but they were blank. "The girl only wrote on the first page."

"Maybe she was afraid someone would read her private thoughts," I replied.

Janie handed me back the diary and continued to dig through the trunk. I read the entry again and flipped through the empty pages. That's when I noticed some of the pages were missing. Torn out. Did the girl tear out the pages, or did someone else?

"Janie, some of the pages from the diary are missing," I said.

My cousin ignored me. She was staring down at a picture, her face filled with a kind of fear I had never seen before.

I took the picture from her hands and realized what had frightened her. The girl in the photograph wore a faded plaid dress with dusty boots. Next to her was a younger boy in a tucked-in shirt, pants that were too short, and a big smile.

The same boy who had appeared on the church steps at Creek Church.

The same boy who had smiled at us and disappeared into the woods.

The same boy who had thrown rocks at my window after midnight and whose eyes glowed silver.

Janie and I huddled together in the humid room. A sharp prick of cool air wedged between my shoulders. Turning the picture around, I saw the same frilly handwriting as in the diary.

"Sophie and Abner Hopkins," I whispered.

"Mrs. Whitney must know who these people are," Janie said.

We both jumped as we heard footsteps on the attic stairs, but it was too late for us to move or cover up our meddling.

Mama appeared. "Are you girls almost finished?"

Janie sprang up. "Yes, Aunt Delilah. We just need to put some stuff back, and then we'll be down."

I pointed to the two bags full of Granddaddy Greene's clothes. "I found some nice suits and ties for the clothing drive."

Mama didn't seem to notice our guilty faces. "Great. When you're done, come on down. We'll be leaving soon."

Janie and I hurriedly put everything back in the

trunk, and Janie placed the lock back together with a tiny click. I lugged my bags full of Granddaddy Greene's clothes.

Why did Mrs. Greene have a picture of the ghost boy in a locked trunk? And who was the girl who wrote in the diary? Even if Mrs. Greene knew who they were, I was pretty sure she was keeping those items locked up in the attic on purpose.

CHAPTER TWENTY-FIVE
Blood Kin

When we got back to the house, Mama went into her office to work on one of her court cases. Daddy still hadn't returned with the boys from basketball camp, so Janie and I took this opportunity to visit Mrs. Whitney.

We were disappointed when we got there and found both the gift shop and the history center with CLOSED signs in the windows.

"Do you think she has an appointment?" Janie asked.

I shaded my eyes from the sun and scanned Town Square. Two elderly women browsed a clothing rack outside of Lucille's Consignment Shop. Sunnie was sweeping the sidewalk in front of Loren's Grocery.

Mr. Hawkins was putting two large pieces of lumber into a customer's pickup truck. Then I spotted Mrs. Whitney coming out of the post office with a stack of mail. She was wearing one of her long white dresses, the fabric glowing off her brown skin. Mrs. Whitney opened an umbrella to shield her from the afternoon sun. When she saw us, she paused before continuing her walk. We decided to wave, and she returned the courtesy.

"That's a good sign," Janie said.

We waited for Mrs. Whitney to open the history center door and go inside before we made any moves. The clang of a cowbell on the door announced our arrival. Unlike in the gift shop, Mrs. Whitney had kept everything intact from the original train depot. Two rows of creaky pine benches and a long counter separated the lobby from the back rooms.

Mrs. Whitney was sitting on one of the benches, waiting for us. "Did you come visit me to learn some history?"

"When we had our appointment, we didn't tell you everything," I spurted out.

"We were the ones who woke up the haints at Creek Church," Janie quickly added.

"You think I didn't know that?" Mrs. Whitney

chuckled. Janie and I exchanged confused looks. "I knew you would be back."

"Do you know anyone named Sophie and Abner Hopkins?" I asked.

She stood up from the bench. "Come with me."

We followed Mrs. Whitney as she took us behind the counter and down a hallway to an open room. Names spanned the far wall from the baseboard to the ceiling. They had been hand painted in careful and elegant script. Stark white against midnight-blue paint.

I walked into the room and stared. Janie traced her fingers over one of the names. "Who are all these people?" she asked.

"Names of the victims lynched in Fairfield County," Mrs. Whitney said.

Janie jerked her hand away. Mrs. Whitney gazed at both of us for a moment before she spoke again. "Folks in Warrenville and Alton—both white and black—want to move on, forget about what happened to these people, but I won't ever let them forget their names. Their deaths should never be overlooked. They are an important part of the history of our town."

We followed Mrs. Whitney into another room off

to the left, with thick green carpet. She went to a cabinet and pulled out a display drawer. The glass cover reminded me of the butterfly cases I had seen at the science museum. Several old pictures lay on top of velvet.

Mrs. Whitney pointed to a picture of a dark-skinned woman posing in a fancy coat with a fur trim. "Laura Hamilton was a teacher who taught the sharecropper children in Warrenville. They couldn't go to school with the white children in Alton. The county didn't build a school for us until 1948."

I wondered why the woman's name sounded so familiar, and then I remembered. Miss Hamilton was the teacher who had given Sophie the diary.

Mrs. Whitney pointed to another picture. "This is the 1947 Warrenville Colored School class."

The children stood in three rows beside Miss Hamilton. They were smiling despite their lack of shoes, raggedy clothing, and dirty faces. In the front row, a small boy held the hand of an older girl beside him. They looked like an exact copy of the picture we saw in Mrs. Greene's attic.

Janie bent down and touched the glass. "We saw this boy at Creek Church."

Mrs. Whitney didn't seem surprised. "That's Abner Hopkins and his older sister Sophie."

"What happened to him?" Nervous energy pressed against my chest. I controlled the rapid beating of my heart by taking a deep breath. The hairs on the back of my neck stood up as we waited to hear what Mrs. Whitney was about to say. I thought of the names on the midnight-blue wall. The same color as the night sky. Would I see Abner's name like a lost star? Was he a part of Warrenville's dark history?

"No one knows," Mrs. Whitney said. "He disappeared without a trace."

"They never found him?" Janie asked.

"The boy is a restless spirit, so I'm certain he met a tragic end," she said. "Quite common during that time. There are no known records of his passing."

Janie and I looked at each other, stricken by Mrs. Whitney's casual tone. She must have noticed. "Has anyone told you about the sharecropper farm, Shiloh?"

We both shook our heads, afraid to speak.

Mrs. Whitney went back to the cabinet and pulled out another display drawer. She pointed to a picture of two men. The older man sat in a chair and had pale skin and blond hair. He wore a dark suit and held a Bible. The younger man stood beside him; his light eyes were lifeless and cold. I felt a twinge of uneasiness.

"This is Lucius Alcott and his son Evern." Mrs. Whitney pointed to the men in the picture. "Back in the day, Lucius's grandfather operated Shiloh as a plantation. After the Civil War, the former slaves sharecropped the land.

"Abner's father was named Jack. Lucius and Jack grew up together, knew each other since birth. Lucius had promised to give Jack and some of the other sharecroppers the land they worked on day in and day out. No one had heard of that before, but Lucius was different from most white men in Fairfield County at the time.

"But when Jack was killed in an accident, Abner became proxy to the promise of his father's land. Lucius's son Evern was none too pleased. A lot of white folks in this area didn't like it either. They used fear and violence to keep the sharecroppers in their place."

"So Abner was promised the land, but no one wanted him to have it?" I asked.

Mrs. Whitney nodded. "It wasn't too long after that Abner went missing. Several witnesses saw Abner get into a truck with Evern and with his friends, but Evern claimed the boy ran away."

"Why didn't anyone do anything?" Janie asked.

"What could they do? Back then a white man's word was trusted over anything else." Mrs. Whitney's eyes had a sad, faraway look. "Broke poor Lucius's heart. He died soon after."

"Is this around the time the Klan burned down the church?" I asked.

"After the community protested in Alton for the police chief to search for the boy, Evern and his friends torched Creek Church as a warning. At the time Evern was the grand wizard of the Klan in Fairfield County."

Mrs. Whitney's eyes grew dark as she traveled to the past. "Creek Church was a place of worship. A safe haven. But the Klan turned it into something else. A place of terror. A place these men decided to turn into a shrine of their hate."

"What happened after that?" Janie asked tentatively.

"These were hard choices to make. Things were changing but not fast enough. The community in Warrenville had to make a choice: live in violence or suffer in peace. Both choices came with sacrifices. Evern continued to mistreat the sharecroppers. Cheated them out of their crops and wages. Never gave them the land they were promised. A lot of families left and went up north. Without the cheap labor to keep the land going, Evern ended up selling most of it. In the end, he lost everything and died without a penny to his name."

"What happened to Sophie?" I asked.

"She settled in Warrenville. Took up as a seamstress and got married. But soon after, she turned ill and died young."

I thought of the possible reasons Mrs. Greene would have Sophie's diary and family pictures in the attic. I thought of the principle of Occam's razor. Sometimes the most simple and obvious explanation is the right one.

"We found a picture of Sophie and Abner in my grandma's attic. We also found Sophie's diary."

I thought of Abner's human form versus the shadows I had seen at Creek Church and outside my window. "Do haints only reveal themselves to blood kin?"

"Very good, Sarah." Mrs. Whitney smiled at me. "Sophie was your grandma's mama."

So Abner had been trying to communicate with us, not scare us! It was all starting to make sense.

"You also said blood kin can put a spirit to rest. Can we help him?" I asked.

"Such horrid things have happened at Creek Church," Mrs. Whitney said. "I'm sure you know by now Abner isn't the only spirit that dwells in that place. Those killed by the evil intentions of men have become evil themselves. Their hatred keeps them bound to this world. I believe it would be hard for anything good to remain there without succumbing to the evil."

"But you said the haints were just restless," Janie said.

"Most spirits are harmless. Others have different intentions. Which is why I gave you the extra protection," she replied.

"But Abner isn't evil," I said.

"Not yet," she added.

Mrs. Whitney returned the pictures to the cabinet. Janie and I looked at each other. The haints surrounded Abner's light with their darkness. There had to be some way, as his family, we could help him.

"I'm going to talk to your grandma about this. My hope is that she'll come around," Mrs. Whitney said.

"When do you plan on speaking with her?" I asked. "Should we be there with you?"

Mrs. Whitney gave us a look. "Not a good idea. I

would also suggest you keep what you found out to yourselves. If she finds out you were up in her attic, picking through her things, she won't be happy."

"Aren't you worried about Abner turning evil?" Janie asked. "Shouldn't we do something before that happens?"

Mrs. Whitney placed her arms on our shoulders and ushered us out of the room. "Girls, I have a plan to get our community to help. No need to worry."

"We could still help you," I said.

"This is something that should involve grown folks." She eyed us closely. "Don't worry, girls. I do have a plan. All the Warrenville spirits will be released once and for all." Mrs. Whitney's voice was different, stronger and defiant. "The past will not claim these souls. Not as long as I'm still breathing."

When we arrived home, Jasper and Ellis were eating ham sandwiches in the den. Mama was still in her office, working on her court case.

"Where's Daddy?" I asked Ellis.

"He's upstairs taking an old-man nap." Ellis mashed the rest of his sandwich into his mouth.

"We have something important to tell you," Janie said.

The boys looked confused as we sat down between them on the couch. "It's about the boy we saw at Creek Church. We found a picture of him in Mrs. Greene's attic. From 1947!"

Jasper stopped eating. "Wait. What? So this means he's been haunting Creek Church for over seventy years? Start from the beginning."

So we did. We told them about the history of the Shiloh farm, the Alcott family, the violence of the Klan, and our family bond to Abner and Sophie Hopkins.

"Mrs. Whitney thinks he was murdered?" Jasper asked.

Janie nodded. "She didn't exactly say that, but she thinks he met a bad end."

I kept going back to the picture of Evern Alcott and his dead, flat eyes. I didn't understand how someone could harm a little boy, but then I remembered the words in Sophie's diary: *We are not seen as human.*

"So if Sophie is our great-grandma, how come we don't know nothing about her?" Ellis asked.

I thought of Mrs. Greene and how she kept those items locked in a trunk in the attic. Full of memories of her family. She had put them in a corner of throwaway, forgotten things. Just like Granddaddy

Greene's belongings. Maybe she wanted to protect us from what had happened in our family history. Mrs. Whitney said the past couldn't be changed, but we were finding out how important it was for it not to be forgotten.

"You know Mrs. Greene never talks about her family," I said. "Now we know why. What happened to Abner was awful."

"Did you see the Wall of Remembrance?" Jasper asked.

I nodded. My shoulders felt like a force was pushing down on me, the weight of all the names I had seen. So many names. So many people hurt.

"When she first started painting them, she was afraid the wall wouldn't be big enough," he said.

As we grew up, Daddy had told us about Warrenville's past and how our community fought against Jim Crow and survived terror from the Klan. I knew it was important to know these things even if I hadn't experienced them. Warrenville was my home, a place where I could roam around without fear of being harmed. But it hadn't always been this way, and it was a blessing I had taken for granted.

"Mrs. Whitney says she's gonna ask Mrs. Greene for help," I said.

Mama opened the French doors and came out of the office. When she walked into the den, we all fell silent. "You all having a secret meeting or something?"

"We were just telling the boys about what we saw at the History Center," Janie said. "You were right, Aunt Delilah. Mrs. Whitney knows a lot about Warrenville."

"That's great to hear. I need to make time to go there myself to see what she's gathered." Mama disappeared into the kitchen.

Jasper leaned closer to us. "You think she can convince Mrs. Greene?"

"Our grandma ain't gonna help a root witch," Ellis said. "I can tell you that already."

"Mrs. Whitney says she has a plan," I said.

Janie frowned. "A plan that she's keeping secret. We have no idea what it is. She wouldn't tell us. She won't even let us help."

"I want to trust Mrs. Whitney," I said. "If she has a plan, then we need to believe her."

CHAPTER TWENTY-SIX
Heritage Festival

Every third Saturday in July, the townsfolk of Warrenville came together and celebrated the community at the Heritage Festival. Even far-flung kin returned home to reconnect with their roots. It was a family homecoming filled with memories and laughter. Located in Marigold Park, each festival booth boasted homemade crafts, art, and specialty food. Kids sat on folding chairs, getting their faces painted, while others walked around with huge clouds of cotton candy or corn dogs on big sticks.

We went to Town Square as a family. Mama and Daddy held hands as they walked down to Main Street. Ellis, Janie, and I strode ahead and practiced our balance on the narrow iron beams of the railroad tracks near the Train Depot.

"Can I get something to eat?" Ellis asked.

Daddy pulled out a few dollar bills from his pocket and gave them to my brother. "This is all you're getting. Make good decisions."

Ellis's face opened up into a huge grin, and he rushed toward the funnel cake booth.

Mama and Daddy stopped to talk with some neighbors, so Janie and I ventured into the crowd to explore before it was time to help Mrs. Greene. We split up to browse the booths. Mrs. Folet sold jewelry with feathers from her peacock farm. Dante Smith passed out personally recorded gospel music. Mr. Hopewell displayed his oil and watercolor art of Warrenville landmarks. I stopped and stared at a small painting.

"You like it?" Mr. Hopewell rubbed his beard, stark white against his brown skin. His eyes focused on me. "That's Creek Church back in the day."

I picked up the painting for a closer look and could now see the stone steps leading the way to a door. I imagined wooden pews and a small pulpit for the pastor. Then all of a sudden I saw the church in flames. White planks singeing black, embers·lighting up the night. Pale faces in the amber glow watching the church burn. I placed the painting back on the table.

"You interested in buying it? I can give you a discount on account of your mama," he said. "She helped me when those white folks tried to take my pension."

"I'll think about it and come back. Thank you, Mr. Hopewell."

Janie and I finally met back up at the Deaconess Board booth. Several desserts were on display, but everyone wanted a slice of Mrs. Greene's red velvet cake.

Our grandma promptly held out our aprons. "Y'all are late."

"Sorry," I mumbled.

We sliced cake and wrapped up pies. Mrs. Greene beamed every time someone complimented her on her baking skills.

Pastor Munroe stopped by the booth. "My wife adores your red velvet cake. Thank you so much for setting one aside for us."

"My pleasure," Mrs. Greene said.

"So are you going to follow in your grandma's footsteps? Be a renowned baker?" he asked me.

"Sarah is going to be an astronaut," Janie said.

Pastor Munroe stepped back impressed. "Is that right, now?"

"Actually I'm going to be an astrobiologist," I corrected Janie.

"With God's love, anything is possible." He squeezed my hand. "Stay blessed."

The crowds started to thin, and I spotted Jovita and the Jones Girls. They were coming toward our booth, and I touched Janie's shoulder.

"We've got company."

Janie put on her rotten-egg face, complete with a frown. Jovita and the Jones Girls stopped in front of the booth. Yvonne showcased her wolf grin and looked at us as if we were two tasty snacks.

"Y'all got any more red velvet cake?" she asked.

"Not for you we don't," Janie sneered.

Sheree popped her gum, and Lola rolled her eyes. Jovita rubbed her arms as if she was cold and stared at the dessert on display, avoiding eye contact with me.

"That cake is dry and nasty anyway," Yvonne said. "Folks only come by here because they're trying to be nice."

"Dry and nasty must be your favorite flavor because here you are, asking for a slice," Janie said. "Like I said,

211

we don't sell red velvet cake to mean country birds."

"You better watch yourself," Yvonne taunted. "I don't forget when I've been disrespected."

"Cut it out," Jovita said, a defiant spark in her voice. My old friend was still in there somewhere. Yvonne sucked her teeth but remained silent and gave Janie the stank eye.

Sheree popped her gum again. "You're not gonna give any birthday wishes?"

Jovita made eye contact with me but quickly looked down at her sandals. I didn't understand her. What was she even doing with these girls?

"Happy birthday, Jovita," I said quietly.

She raised her head and gave me a weak smile. "Thanks, Sarah."

"We should go. We need to get ready for your party tonight." Yvonne took Jovita's hand and led her away.

"You're better off without her." Janie leaned against me. "Good riddance."

Mrs. Greene came back into the booth. "Why is Jovita with those girls?"

"We have no idea," Janie said.

When the Deaconess Board booth sold out of cake and pies, we started to clean up. We stopped when we heard a blare of loud static and a voice coming from the Train Depot.

"Excuse me," the voice said. "Excuse me, I need you to gather round. I have something to say."

"It's Mrs. Whitney." I walked out of Marigold Park to the edge of Town Square. Janie trotted behind me and peered over my shoulder.

Mrs. Whitney held a bullhorn in her hand and gestured to a small crowd that had gathered in front of the Train Depot. I saw Mama and Daddy at the back of the crowd. Ellis and Jasper were standing near the front. My brother bit into a funnel cake and cocked his head to listen.

"Now that I have everyone's attention . . ." Mrs. Whitney spoke into the bullhorn, her voice carrying in the wind. "I opened the History Center to document Warrenville's past events so that we can move toward a better future as a community."

Mrs. Greene and the ladies of the Deaconess Board now stood beside us. My grandma crossed her arms and put on her trademark grimace.

"As we celebrate the fiftieth year of this festival, we also need to acknowledge the troubled spirits of your blood kin who were taken from this world by hatred and fear."

"Is this her idea of a plan?" Janie whispered in my ear.

Some people in the crowd looked around confused, others upset, while a few leaned forward to listen more closely. Mrs. Whitney paused. She now had the townsfolk's full attention.

"I want the families of Warrenville to know I am here to help. We have a reckoning in this town, and I can only help usher the restless spirits of your blood kin into the light with your support."

A low grumble traveled through the people. Ellis stopped eating his funnel cake, and Jasper stood with his mouth open.

"Some of you have already come to me with your spiritual problems. I know it can be frightening, but I can provide protection to any family member who needs it," Mrs. Whitney continued. "It's our duty to help these restless spirits transition to the next plane of existence."

A few people shook their heads and started to walk away.

"This is not the place!" a woman shouted.

"Small children are here," another woman yelled. "You're gonna scare them to death!"

Mrs. Whitney pointed to a family in the front. "Delores Cunningham is trapped here in this world. She was a loving mother to you. Don't you want to see her spirit released?"

A woman grabbed her husband and stormed off. Murmurs stirred in their exit. Mrs. Whitney searched the crowd and pointed to another family.

"Titus Williams was going to Alton to vote, and he never made it. Don't you want your grandfather to finally rest in peace?"

"That was in the past!" the man shouted back at her. "Stop dredging up painful memories. You need to let it be." His family turned and also left.

The crowd dwindled as Mrs. Whitney tried to convince more family members, but no one wanted to listen. I saw Mama and Daddy talking to Mr. Coolidge. Mrs. Whitney's fiancé nodded during their conversation, his face grim.

I waited for Mrs. Whitney to say Abner's name through the bullhorn, loud enough for everyone in Warrenville to hear. Maybe in the spotlight of the Heritage Festival, Mrs. Greene would listen. But it never happened. Mr. Coolidge came up next to Mrs. Whitney and took the bullhorn away. She slumped her shoulders in defeat. No family member had taken her up on her offer to save the restless spirits of their blood kin.

The ladies of the Deaconess Board tittered with comments.

"This is exactly why we rejected her application," Mrs. Collins said.

"Such a disgrace," Mrs. Jackson said. "I'm just glad Sylvester had the sense to take that bullhorn away from her."

Janie and I went back to cleaning up the booth; our grandma remained silent as she tidied up and folded tablecloths, her face unreadable. When she finished, she turned to us.

"Find your Daddy so you can head home," she said. "The festival is over."

"We can still do something, you know. We're blood kin," Janie said as we made our way out of Marigold Park. "We can save Abner ourselves."

My cousin had a gleam in her eye, and a new resolve grew in my chest. Mrs. Whitney had told us that haints could be dangerous, but she also had given me Daphnis. We needed to find a way to communicate with Abner and save him before it was too late. We could help Mrs. Whitney bring the town together. We just needed to convince the townsfolk to listen. Maybe if we saved Abner, then others would want to save their blood kin too.

I remembered the slim book I had found in the library: the woman holding the gilded harp, the full moon's glow highlighting her dark skin. The Witching Hour.

"Maybe there is a way," I said.

CHAPTER TWENTY-SEVEN

Brave Girl

The next day, my parents briefly talked about what had happened at the Heritage Festival. Daddy said Mrs. Whitney had gotten caught up in her tall tales. Mama told us Mrs. Whitney's heart was in the right place, because she wanted to help the Warrenville community. But neither of them believed restless spirits were haunting the town. We didn't try to convince them otherwise.

While Janie painted her nails, I researched the Witching Hour on her phone. I didn't want to go into Mama's office and take the chance of her discovering that I had been searching about it on the computer.

From the information I gathered, there was a

consensus that the Witching Hour was a time associated with supernatural activity, but the timing of when that hour happened differed. Most agreed that it could be anywhere from midnight to three in the morning. A full moon provided the highest energy for communication with spirits. I decided to take copious notes and cross-reference my findings.

I also searched for more information on *The Witch's Moons* and found the author's website. In her photo, Lucinda Meadow wore a dark dress, which highlighted her pale skin. Most of the information she provided online was the same as in her book. She also had some of the witch illustrations on her site. I scrolled down until I found the dark woman in the red silk gown. I stared at the gilded harp in her arms.

At the end of her explanation of why she wrote the book, Lucinda Meadow simply stated: *In the end, it is only our beliefs that matter.*

My beliefs had changed. I now believed in ghosts. I had no choice. The evidence was too overwhelming. However, science still provided me with the facts. The moon's gravitational pull helped with the evolution of life on our planet. The moon regulated the ocean tides and the climate. The moon was powerful, so why couldn't it also provide a way to communicate with another realm? Why couldn't the moon lift the veil to the spirit world?

"Did you find anything?" Janie asked.

I turned to face her. "I think I did."

That night Jasper came for a sleepover and family movie night. Daddy let Ellis pick out a doomsday thriller where the oceans flooded all the cities and everyone fought to get passage on a government cruise ship.

When we finished the movie, I brought everyone into my room. I sat at my desk, holding Daphnis in my lap. Janie nuzzled Walter, who sat on her shoulder. Jasper and Ellis were on the floor in front of me. My brother brought a bowl of potato chips like he was about to watch another movie. When Janie tried to reach in for a snack, Ellis smacked her hand.

"Get your own food," Ellis said.

Janie frowned. "It's probably nasty anyway. Your boy breath has been all over it."

"So what's up, Sarah?" Jasper asked.

I hoped that what I was about to say wouldn't scare them. I needed their help. There was no way I was going to Creek Church by myself at night.

"I figured out a way we can help Abner. I've

calculated the best time to communicate with him."

Jasper eyed me suspiciously. "You're not gonna let Mrs. Whitney handle this? She said haints can be dangerous. We don't want a repeat of what happened the last time we were at Creek Church."

"We still have some blessed salt and the protection pouches Mrs. Whitney gave us. Plus, I have Daphnis," I said.

"Who?" Ellis asked.

I gave the statue to my brother, and he examined it closely.

"She's a talisman Mrs. Whitney gave me," I told him.

"Daphnis is one of the main reasons the haints haven't returned to the house," Janie added.

"So there's a special time to communicate with haints?" Jasper asked.

"It's called the Witching Hour. During a full moon at midnight—"

"You're kidding, right?" Ellis asked.

"Spirits are at their peak at midnight during a full moon," I said. "The veil between the worlds is at its thinnest."

"How did you figure out all this?" Jasper asked.

"I found a book in the library," I said. "Then I did

some research online. The Witching Hour seems to be our best and only chance to talk with Abner."

"You really believe this?" Jasper asked.

"Duh, if Sarah believes what she read, then it must have some worth," Janie said.

"It has to be during that hour? At midnight?" Jasper grimaced as if his stomach ached.

Ellis shook his head. "I don't wanna be near Creek Church at that time."

"The next full moon is going to occur Friday night. We can go and get Abner out of that place," I said.

"We're forgetting something," Ellis said. "Mama doesn't let us go anywhere after supper. What makes you think she'll let us out at midnight?"

"We're going to tell Mama we're having a camp night at Jasper's house," I said.

Janie perked up. "You've thought of everything, huh?"

"Do you think your mama would let you do that?" Jasper asked.

"If Sarah asks, she'll let us," Ellis said. "But that means she'll have to lie."

"It won't be lying. I do have a tent," Jasper said.

I already knew I needed to be the one to ask Mama. I had never lied to her before, and even though we would have a camp night at Jasper's house, I wouldn't be telling the whole truth.

"It will be easy to sneak away at my place," Jasper said. "My mama's a hard sleeper. After she knocks out, you can have a parade and fireworks, and she won't wake up."

Jasper's daddy also worked the graveyard shift, painting transformers at a manufacturing plant in Alton, so he wouldn't be around either.

"So we're really going to do this? End our lives as haint food?" Ellis asked.

"You don't have to go," Janie said. "You can stay at home."

Ellis pouted and ate the rest of his potato chips in silence.

"It's the right thing to do, Ellis," I said. "This is bigger than us. Abner isn't the only restless spirit. So many others need to be saved. We need to show that it's possible. We need to get people to believe. This is what Mrs. Whitney wanted."

"Sarah's right," Janie said. "This is how we can help the whole town."

"You don't want to ask your mama at the last minute," Jasper said. "We need to get our plans together."

"I don't want to sound suspicious," I added.

"It's not like she's gonna guess," Janie said.

Going to Creek Church during the Witching Hour scared me. The place was creepy enough in the daytime. But I wanted to help Abner and, hopefully, the town, so I would have to find a way to be a brave girl. I would do it for him. I would do it for everyone I called family.

CHAPTER TWENTY-EIGHT
A Guilty Liar

On Monday night I went downstairs to Mama's office. She had the French doors closed and was focused on a mess of papers. Her hair was up in a topknot, her reading glasses perched on her nose. I wanted to turn away and go back upstairs. Mama liked Jasper, so I knew she would let us stay at his house. But I didn't know if I had it in me to stretch the truth about the real reason we wanted to spend the night. I thought about the Witching Hour. Could it be true? That sliver of time when the dead could communicate with the living? What would Abner tell us? What if he didn't show up? I knocked lightly on the door.

Mama looked up and smiled. I quietly went in

and sat down in the leather chair in front of her desk.

"You're still working, Mama?" I asked.

"I have a case I'm researching," she said. "Everything okay?"

"Yes." I fidgeted in my seat. "I just wanted to ask you a question."

"What is it?" Mama took off her glasses. "Do you need to check your e-mail?"

"I was wondering if we could have a camp night at Jasper's house."

"What do you plan to do?" Mama asked.

My stomach lurched, but I continued selling my fabricated story. "Jasper has a tent and wants to spend the night under the stars. He wants to learn more about the constellations. Plus, there's a full moon. I could teach him about the different craters you can see with the naked eye."

"That sounds like fun," she said.

I was surprised at how well this was going. I had been prepared for more cross-examination. Maybe Mama was tired. Or maybe she was glad that we were getting out of the house.

"I was thinking Friday night?"

Mama ruffled through her papers and looked at the desk calendar. "That should work."

"Really?" I said, surprised. "You'll let us go?"

"I don't see why not," Mama said. "Unless there's something else going on?"

I pressed my lips together. *Yes, Mama, we need to communicate with a ghost boy at midnight.*

"No, Mama."

I couldn't tell Mama the truth. She was a logical person who dealt with facts. Just like I used to be. She would want proof, and I couldn't give her any right now.

"Okay," Mama said as she put her reading glasses back on, a signal our conversation was over.

I got up to leave and rubbed my hands on my pajamas to wipe away the guilt sweat.

"Sarah," Mama said.

I turned to face her.

"I'm proud of you this summer. I'm glad that you've made Janie feel at home here. A part of the family. I have to admit I was worried at first, but you've shown me that you are the responsible young lady that I knew you could be. I now know that I can trust you."

I swallowed hard. The guilt rose in my throat and spread across my cheeks. Mama didn't know the truth. I wasn't responsible. I was a liar, and I was doing things behind her back. But I couldn't turn away. Not now. I was too invested. In our family. In our town.

"Thanks, Mama," I said.

I walked out of the office and closed the doors. Janie and Ellis were waiting for me in my bedroom. Janie had Walter in her lap.

"What did she say?" Janie asked.

I sat at my desk. I should have been happy about this, but I wasn't. I should have been relieved, but all I felt was guilty.

"She said we could go," I said.

"I knew you could do it," Janie cheered.

I heard the faint trill of the house phone, and a few moments later Daddy appeared in the doorway.

"Sarah, the phone's for you. It's Jovita."

Janie frowned. "I wouldn't take her call."

"It's okay. Thanks, Daddy." I took the cordless phone from him.

I slowly walked down the stairs and sat on the sofa in the den. I was surprised that Jovita was calling me. I took a deep breath and put the phone up to my ear.

"Hello?"

"Sarah?" Jovita's voice was small and high pitched.

"Jovita? What's wrong?"

"I'm sorry." Her voice was full of tears.

Jovita had ignored me all summer. She had become friends with the same girls who had bullied me for years and had publicly thrown away our friendship at the Alton Mall. Even though she stood up for me at the Heritage Festival, she still hadn't invited me to her birthday party. I didn't know which part she was sorry about.

"I've messed everything up," she continued. "Those Jones Girls, they're awful. All they do is talk about people. And then I—" Her voice cracked.

"Jovita, what happened?"

"I—I overheard them," she said. "They were talking about me."

"What did they say?"

"They're not nice. They were using me. They don't even like me."

Jovita had always wanted to be well liked and have lots of friends. She didn't want to be on the outer rim. It was too far away. Too cold and isolated. She wanted to be in the spotlight. To bask in the brightness of attention. As close to the sun as Mercury. But apparently she veered too close and got burned. I listened as Jovita cried on the phone.

I was sad they'd hurt her, but she'd hurt me, too.

"I hope that you can forgive me," she sniffed.

Mama always told me forgiveness was not for the other person but for yourself. Maybe Jovita thought being popular would be more fun than hanging out with me. I know what Janie would do. She wouldn't forgive her. Janie would turn away. But I couldn't. Jovita had been my best friend. The one person *not* in my family I could be myself around. She had made a mistake, and now she was apologizing. Her sadness was real, and it was a feeling I knew too well.

"Jovita, I didn't know what to think when you stopped talking to me. When I saw you with the Jones Girls . . . it really hurt."

She let out a shaky sigh. "I know. I'm really sorry."

"I forgive you," I said. "But I don't know. So much has happened."

Jovita was quiet for a moment. "I understand, but . . . can I make it up to you? Do you want to come to my house Friday night? We could have a slumber party. You can even bring your cousin if you want."

"I already have plans," I said.

"Oh." Jovita's voice dropped in disappointment.

"Maybe another time?" I asked.

"Yeah, okay," she said.

Silence crackled on the phone. Was Jovita my friend again? Would I be able to tell her what had happened since we last talked? Or saw each other? Would she believe me about Abner?

"I better go, but I'll talk to you later," I said.

I did feel sorry for Jovita, and I hated that she had to find out the hard way about the Jones Girls. I didn't know if we could still be as close now. I had more stuff in common with Janie. She didn't ignore me, and she believed in Abner.

Jovita would have to wait. I had bigger fish to fry.

CHAPTER TWENTY-NINE

Witching Hour

On Friday night we put our sleeping bags into the trunk of Mama's car. She had bought them as a surprise for us, and I felt even guiltier.

"Remember, it's not lying," Janie said. "We technically are spending the night at Jasper's house."

"You better hope she never finds out about any of the other parts either." Ellis pushed his overnight bag in the trunk. The bag of blessed salt was inside.

"Do you have your pouches?" I asked them.

Ellis and Janie nodded. I reached into my pocket and squeezed my amulet. We needed all the protection we could get.

Mama appeared on the porch in a sundress. Daddy was taking her into Alton for a date night.

Her hair was in a tight twist, and she had on shimmery eye shadow. Her dark brown skin glowed in the sunset. I hoped I would look as pretty as Mama when I grew up.

"Are we ready to go?" she asked.

"Yes, Mama." Ellis slammed the trunk.

When we arrived at the trailer, Jasper and his daddy were fixing up the tent.

"At least it looks like we're having a camp night, even though we're gonna die at Creek Church," Ellis whispered to me.

"Nobody's going to die," I said.

Mama rolled down her window. "Jasper, what a lovely tent."

"Thanks, Mrs. Greene," Jasper said.

We all winced at Jasper's mistake.

"I've told him a thousand times it's Mrs. *Duncan*-Greene." Ellis shook his head.

"Is your mother here?" Mama asked.

"Y-yes, ma'am," Jasper stumbled. "You want me to get her?"

"No, that's all right. I think I'll go in for a second." Mama opened the door and turned to us. "Stay here."

We watched her go inside the trailer. After the door closed, Jasper leaned inside the car.

"Does she suspect something?" he asked.

"I don't think so," Janie said. "I think she's happy to be going on an adult date."

We were acting as normal as we could. When a few more moments passed, I began to worry. Then the trailer door opened, and Mama and Mrs. Johnson came out wearing big smiles on their faces. They hugged each other, and Mrs. Johnson waved to us. She had on a housecoat, and her hair was in pink sponge rollers. Mama motioned to us to get out of the car.

"I'm sorry. Karleen and I started talking about things, and I lost track of time. You kids have fun." She kissed everyone good-bye on the forehead.

I watched Mama drive away, hoping to see her again in the morning.

Jasper's mama made us baked chicken with butter beans, and although Janie, Ellis, and I had already had supper, we left nothing but bones and grease on our plate. I rubbed my tight tummy and sighed.

When darkness fell, we sat outside the tent. The moon was rising in the sky, big and full like a

fluorescent snow globe. I pointed out the faint constellations to Jasper and Ellis. I showed them Scorpius
with its claws pointing north and Sagittarius with its
squat kettle shape. I pointed to the blue star Vega
and her neighbors Deneb and Altair that formed the
Summer Triangle.

"I know constellations too," Ellis said. "That's the
Big Dipper. See it?"

"Yes. That's Ursa Major," I said. "And directly
across from that? That's Polaris. The North Star."

"What time is it?" Janie asked. I don't think she
was entertained by our stargazing.

The lights in the trailer had gone off about an
hour ago. Jasper's mama was hopefully asleep, and if
he was right, she wouldn't wake up until the morning.

"It's almost a half past eleven, so I guess we
should leave." Jasper stood and brushed the grass off
his knees.

"Let me get the salt." Ellis pulled out the sack,
and we got our plastic bags.

"We better take the bag with us," Jasper said after
Ellis had given everyone two handfuls. "Just in case."

"You think it will be that bad?" Ellis asked.

"Better safe than sorry." Janie poured an extra

handful into her plastic bag before she slipped on her backpack.

"She's right," I agreed.

Ellis nodded. "You won't hear no complaining from me."

We walked out of Beaverdam Trailer Park, turned on our flashlights, and ventured down Hardeman Road in the dark. The sound of crickets was thick in the air, and the moon was high above us. My flashlight had new batteries, and I pointed its bright light in the direction of any sound. Luckily, I had only seen three possums so far.

We approached Linnard Run and stood in front of the dirt path. The NO TRESPASSING sign was draped in darkness. The two leaning posts looked like dark smears. My neck itched with fear, and my heart tightened in my chest.

"It's not too late to turn back," Ellis reminded us.

"We've come this far," Janie said. "Let's keep going."

The sound of my steady heartbeat pounded in my ears as we walked along the silent dirt road. I kept holding my breath and forced myself to inhale deeply. The night breeze had gotten stronger, and chills rippled across my skin.

"It's getting colder," Janie said.

Farther down Linnard Run, the brightness of the moon spilled over everything, casting a misty glow. At first I was relieved, but then I noticed that the light wasn't coming from the moon.

"Where's that light coming from?" My brother's voice was an octave higher than usual.

"It's coming from Creek Church," Jasper said.

"Ghost light," Ellis added. "Great."

"What time is it?" Janie whispered.

I checked my watch. "It's not yet midnight."

When we arrived at Creek Church, an eerie blue-white light filtered through the trees. Dense fog hung in the air, and tiny sparks of lightning appeared. We stood and stared. Even Janie was silent.

"Do y'all see that?" Ellis whispered.

The fog swirled and thickened, growing darker as the night breeze moved through the leaves. Our breaths formed small white puffs in the air as the branches creaked.

"Quick," I said. "We need to make a salt circle."

We grabbed salt from our plastic bags and poured it around us. Through the fog, we could see the shadows standing in the woods. My eyes widened. Haints with glowing silver eyes surrounded us; their whispers clamored in the air. It was entirely different from seeing them outside my window. We were dumb for coming here and thinking we could handle this.

"Don't move," Janie warned.

Even if I wanted to run, I couldn't. I was frozen with fear. The haints shimmered in the blue-white light. One by one, they floated across the stone slab and loomed above the church steps.

"Stay in the circle," Janie said, her voice low.

"They're going to get us!" Ellis shrieked as he tried to break free.

Jasper held him still. "Trust me—you do not want to go outside this circle."

The haints whispers grew angrier.

"What are they saying?" Janie asked.

"Be quiet," I whisper yelled.

The haints moaned, filling my whole body with an aching sadness; tears brimmed from my eyes. The shadows propelled themselves down the church steps and melted through the weeds. We grabbed one another's hands as they moved closer. The coldness made my teeth chatter. It was then that I heard what they were saying. Not words. They were saying names.

Clinton Chambers

Minnie Ivory

Felix Cremer

Lacy Mitchell

Lint Shaw

So many names. They hovered around us chanting them. I wanted to put my hands to my ears to drown them out. But then just as soon as it began, the whispering stopped. The haints floated around our salt circle. They hadn't touched us. They hadn't hurt us. Our protection had worked. We watched them disappear down Linnard Run.

I let go of Janie's hand. She had been crying too. The boys sniffed and wiped their noses.

"What happened?" Ellis asked. "Why did they leave?"

"Maybe they're not looking for us? Maybe they're searching for the people who killed them?" Jasper said.

"Well, they won't find them," I replied.

Deep within the darkness of the woods, another shadow appeared. Unlike the haints, the boy didn't look like a ghost. He had on his ragged shirt and pants with no shoes.

We stood and stared at Abner.

CHAPTER THIRTY

Abner's Dream

So you can see him?" I asked Jasper.

"Yes, I see him." Jasper walked out of the salt circle. "It must be because of the Witching Hour, right?"

The moon came out from behind the clouds and covered the woods with pale light. Our shadows spread like tall mutant trees with moving limbs.

"We came back to see you," Janie stated calmly.

Abner glanced at the trees, now still. He stood there, then turned and dropped from the church slab to walk back into the woods, his shadow a ray of blue white in the darkness.

"We should follow him," I said.

It wasn't until we were halfway to the graveyard

that I noticed the black tree. The branches were covered with green leaves that glowed in the moonlight. Its bark was healthy and strong.

"Do you see that?" Janie pointed at the tree.

We stood a few steps behind and watched Abner. He was at the far end of the graveyard. He paused to stare at the ground, then continued farther into the woods.

"He's searching for something," I whispered as we followed.

Abner continued to walk but stopped to search the area again. Then he disappeared.

"Where did he go?!" Janie asked.

"What now?" Ellis whined.

"Be quiet." Jasper held up his hand. "Do you hear that noise?"

We strained to listen. At first it sounded like unsettled wind, but it was someone gasping. The faint sounds of metal scraping against stone filled the air.

"Where's it coming from?" Ellis asked.

A dense fog appeared between us. Tendrils of smoke curled from the ground and floated upward. The moonlight caused the smoke to glow light yellow. We huddled close and moved behind the thick trunk of a sycamore tree.

"Is it the haints?" Ellis reached into the bag of salt.

"I don't think so," I said. "It's coming from the ground."

Out of the mist the dark figure of a man emerged. He dragged a large burlap sack. Attached to the sack was a shovel, which scraped across the rocks. The man didn't seem to see us. He wiped his brow and brushed his blond hair out of his eyes. He wore trousers and a shirt rolled high to the elbows, revealing pale skin. He had the same glow as Abner.

I swallowed hard. "It's another ghost."

"How many does that make?" Ellis asked.

"Shh. What's he doing?" Janie moved forward.

Jasper held Janie by her backpack to prevent her from getting any closer. "I think we're about to find out."

As the fog lightened, the details of the man became clear. I gasped when I recognized who he was.

"What's his ghost doing out here?" Janie's eyes widened in shock.

"You know who that is?" Jasper asked.

"It's Evern Alcott," I said, voice trembling.

Evern cut the rope around the bag. When it opened, the contents inside spilled out onto the ground. I put my hand to my mouth. It was the body of a boy in a cotton shirt and torn trousers. It was Abner.

Evern walked a couple more paces before stopping, and then he began to dig. When he was finished, he pushed Abner into the hole with his shovel. His laughter made the hairs on my neck stand up. He covered the hole with dirt. Then he covered the spot with old leaves.

"Nobody will think to look for ya here!" His laughter brought chills to my skin; it felt like a bucket of water had been dumped over my body. Slowly Evern's ghost disappeared with the mist.

I ran to the spot where Evern had dug the grave. "This is where he's been all these years. Hidden in plain sight."

"Did you see?" said a voice from behind us.

Ellis yelped, and I swirled around to see Abner. He was sitting on the ground, his hands in his lap. Up close, he didn't seem as real, more like a hologram, but his eyes were brown and sad.

"I wanted to show you what happened," Abner said. "I only remember waking up here. No one has ever come to see."

I thought I would be scared, but I wasn't. This was my blood kin. He wasn't a scary haint but a lost little boy. I could see the fear in Jasper's eyes, but he didn't leave us. Ellis even stood guard with his slingshot, proving his bravery. Janie and I moved closer and sat down in front of Abner.

"Do you know who I am?" I asked him.

Abner looked at me, but there was no recognition in his eyes. "Do you know my sister Sophie?"

"We do," Janie said. "She's family, which means you're our family too."

"Why hasn't she come to get me? Ever since I woke up, I've been waiting. She told me if I got lost that she would find me," he said.

"She's not here anymore, but we can help you," I said.

"Where did she go?" Abner asked.

"We can take you to her," Janie said. "You just need to come with us. It isn't safe for you. You don't belong here."

Abner bowed his head and started to cry. "I just want to go home."

Janie and I looked at each other. I wasn't sure what to do next. Should we take him to Sophie's grave? To Mrs. Whitney? Maybe my plan wasn't as great as I had thought.

"Hey, y'all, I think time is running out." Ellis

pointed to the trees. The mist was returning.

"Abner, we can take you home," I said, hoping a better idea would come to me along the way. "We can take you to Sophie."

A loud gust of wind brought down a nearby tree branch, and angry hisses filled the air. Abner stopped crying and raised his head. His eyes were no longer brown and sad. Now they glowed bright silver. Janie and I scrambled away as Abner floated upward. The blue-white glow drained from his form, and he transformed into a long dark shadow.

"This is my home now," he said, his voice cold and distant, before he disappeared.

"We need to leave!" Jasper yelled.

"Wait!" I said. "We have to mark his grave. We'll never find it again if we don't."

"Put some salt around the spot to mark it," Janie ordered.

"If I do that, we won't have anymore left." Ellis's voice cracked.

"Do it, Ellis!" Janie yelled.

My brother emptied the bag of salt and quickly put a ring of it around the spot where Abner was buried. Almost immediately, the salt disappeared into the ground.

"What just happened?!" Ellis shouted.

"We have to mark it another way," I said. "Find some rocks. Sticks. Anything."

We scrambled to find rocks and piled them on top of one another. The mist grew thicker. Leaves rustled, and the dark shapes spread out above them. After a short hesitation, I took Daphnis out of my pocket and put it on top of the rocks. Maybe she could protect Abner.

"We don't have any salt left," Ellis said. "We can't make another circle."

"What about the salt circle in the road?" Janie asked over the howling wind.

"We need to make a run for it," Jasper said.

I positioned into a runner's lunge. "On the count of three."

We scattered through the graveyard. A roar whipped through my clothes, and I coughed from the coldness caught in my throat. We raced through the woods, sliding on slick leaves. We ran until we reached the broken-chain entrance of Linnard Run.

The shadows hadn't followed us.

"If I never see another haint again it will be too soon," Ellis panted.

"Now we know why he's been haunting Creek Church," Jasper said. "He's buried there."

"Evern did kill him." Janie frowned.

"We woke him up, but I think we also woke up something else," I said. "He's changing. We need to get him out of there before it's too late."

"So we go back," Janie said. "We know where his grave is now. All we need are some shovels and—"

"You want to dig him up?! Haven't we had enough excitement tonight?" Ellis hugged the empty bag of salt.

"We need to get to Jasper's house," I said. "We don't want Jasper's mama to wake up and find us gone."

And with that, we rushed back to the Beaverdam Trailer Park.

CHAPTER THIRTY-ONE
A Solid Plan

When we got back to Jasper's tent, all the lights were still out in his trailer. We let out a collective sigh of relief and dropped our flashlights on the picnic table. Nobody said anything. Janie stared off into space with teary eyes. Jasper held his head in his hands. Ellis wiped his nose with his shirt. My trembling fingers were still cold as ice.

I looked up at the sky. The moon was full and bright. It was at its highest point and would now make the gradual fall into the west. Abner had lived under this same moon. Did he ever wonder about its beauty or where it came from? Did he know that the moon's highest mountain was Mons Huygens? He probably didn't. Unlike me, he wasn't surrounded by astronomy books. But I would like to think he marveled at the moon, the stars, and the universe. I hoped he had found joy when he was alive on this earth.

One day I wanted to discover life on another planet, but tonight I discovered death right here. We had uncovered one of Warrenville's darkest secrets.

Could I tell this to Mama? Should I? She would use her lawyer skills and prepare litigation. She would want to go after the Alcott estate and make an argument for a civil case. But there wasn't an Alcott estate. There wasn't a Shiloh anymore. The Alcotts had long been dead. There was no one left to punish. The only thing left was the restless spirit of a little boy.

Would Mama even believe in all of this? People in Warrenville talked about haints, but did they really have faith in what Mrs. Whitney said? She had pleaded with them at the Heritage Festival, and the townsfolk had turned their backs.

Janie moved beside me. Her eyes were dry now, and they burned with a new resolve. "We have to go back, Sarah," she said.

"I need to process all of this first."

"Sarah, we found out what happened. We need to help him. We're all he has left."

"When the haints came into the road . . . did you recognize any of the names? From the Wall of Remembrance?" I asked.

Janie closed her eyes. "I can't remember any of the names I saw on the wall. There were too many." She took my hand and squeezed it. "This is why it's so important. Maybe then the rest of the town will pay attention."

"Haven't we done enough?" Ellis whined.

"Janie's right. We have to do something," Jasper said.

"Like what?" Ellis protested. "Last time I checked, we were kids."

"We should dig him up," Janie said.

"I ain't digging up no bones!" Ellis cried.

"Nobody asked you!" Janie screeched.

"Shhh," Jasper said. "Keep it down already. You're gonna wake the whole trailer park up."

Ellis shook his head. "So you dig him up. What you gonna do then?"

"We give the bones to the police," Janie said.

"And you don't think they won't ask how we got those bones?" I asked.

"Why do you think he showed us where he was buried? He wants us to dig him up," Janie said.

The vision revealed the mystery of Abner's disappearance. Clearly enough for us to mark his grave with rocks. Maybe it was as simple as getting a shovel.

"That may be true. But Abner has been dead a long time. Someone else must have seen something before we came along," I said.

"We can interview everybody in town," Ellis said. "Have you seen haints? Mist? Creepy shadows?"

Janie rolled her eyes. "Let's face it, if someone else saw what we saw, they would have dug him up already. No one else knows about this."

"You can let me know how it works out," Ellis said. "I ain't digging up no haint."

My brother was right. We might not be able to do this by ourselves, but we couldn't leave Abner in that awful place either.

"Let's just try and get some rest and come up with a game plan in the morning," I said.

The next morning, my whole body ached from sleeping on the ground, and my mouth felt raw. The cold had thawed from my fingers, and they tingled back to life. Janie was sleeping next to me, the boys across from us, deep in their sleeping bags. The tent had sagged down lower as we slept, so I had to search for my overnight bag on my hands and knees.

I crept out of the tent and stretched my legs. The sky still was in the predawn darkness and filled with stars. I looked west and saw the full moon setting.

I thought of Abner, woken up from his dream, waiting for Sophie to find him, and had an idea.

Peering back into the tent, I made sure everyone was still fast asleep. Then I crept up on Jasper's bike and started to pedal away from the Beaverdam Trailer Park. I needed to make an early morning visit.

I rode Jasper's bike down Hardeman Road to Mrs. Whitney's house. It was where her brother had lived before he passed away earlier this spring. She had been staying here since she came back to Warrenville.

The sun started to rise as I veered off the paved road to a dirt lane. The small clapboard house was on a plot of land surrounded by fields. A small garden was on one side, and a collection of marigolds and sunflowers was on the other. The porch was full of ferns, petunias, and spider plants. It was one big bouquet.

Mrs. Whitney was outside, sweeping the porch. Dust puffed into the air with each push of her broom. She wore a blue housecoat, her hair tied up in a yellow turban. She fit in perfectly with her garden.

When she saw me coming into the yard, she stopped sweeping and smiled.

"You caught me in the middle of domestic work." She leaned on her broom. "But you're right on time. I need to change the light on my porch, and I need some help."

Mrs. Whitney reached over to a wood table and grabbed a lightbulb. "Get that folding chair for me."

I got off Jasper's bike and retrieved the metal chair. She positioned it under the faulty light. Mrs. Whitney stepped up and reached to unscrew the bulb. "Hold it now. Keep it steady."

I held the chair and stared up as Mrs. Whitney loomed above me. "We know what happened to Abner," I blurted.

The metal chair squeaked, but Mrs. Whitney continued to concentrate on the lightbulb, humming a tune. The new bulb cracked on and glowed like a tiny yellow sun. She stepped down from the chair to face me.

"Don't you want to know how we found out?" I asked her.

After placing the folding chair against the porch rail, Mrs. Whitney guided me to the porch swing. Instead of answering me, she pushed her feet off the floor. We glided through the air, the thick morning breeze warm on my legs.

"I think you're about to tell me anyway, Miss Sarah," she said.

I thought of the haints moaning the names of the dead and how sad I still felt, knowing they'd been trapped for so many years. Even now, my chest felt heavy with the burden. I put my hand over my heart.

"Last night we went to Creek Church during the Witching Hour."

"That's mighty dangerous," Mrs. Whitney said. "And mighty brave."

"Thinking back on it now, it probably wasn't the best plan. We should have told you, but I wanted to see if we could help Abner ourselves. But he wouldn't leave."

"Some spirits are easier to wrangle than others." Mrs. Whitney paused. "This will be my second time trying to help Abner."

"Wait. You've tried before?"

"When I was about your age, maybe a little older, I went to Creek Church," she said. "But I wasn't alone. I had his blood kin with me."

Mrs. Whitney took a lace handkerchief out of her housecoat pocket and blotted her forehead. She twisted the cloth in her hand. "I need a cold drink." She stood up. "Would you like some lemonade?"

I nodded and followed Mrs. Whitney into the house. I sat down on a couch in the front room, which was filled with boxes, each one labeled with Mrs. Whitney's elegant script. After a few moments she appeared, holding a metal tray with a pitcher of lemonade and two glasses that clinked and wobbled with each careful step.

"It's never too early for lemonade." She poured a glass for each of us. I wanted to swallow it in quick gulps, but I took careful sips.

Mrs. Whitney sat down next to me and drank from her glass. She stared at the pitcher for several seconds. Then she looked at me. "Lena found her mama's diary in an old trunk. She knew the Shiloh story well, and I convinced her to go to Creek Church with me."

I thought of Mrs. Greene as a young girl named Lena, someone who was curious and had many adventures. I couldn't connect that girl to the grandma that I knew now.

"As you already know, Creek Church is a scary place. Lena was afraid. I was too." Mrs. Whitney stood up and walked to the window. "We did try to help that boy's spirit, but we failed. Later, I went back with my mama, but we couldn't convince him."

"Because only blood kin can put a spirit to rest?" I asked.

"That's right. I pleaded with Lena, but she wanted nothing more to do with it. I gave her protective charms, but she claimed they were evil and threw them out. In a fit of rage, she even tore out pages from her mama's diary and burned them. After that, we stopped being friends. Then I got married and moved away, but I still thought about those spirits trapped there." Mrs. Whitney let out a heavy sigh. The sound was loud in the quiet room. "It was one of the reasons I came back. I haven't forgotten them."

"During the Witching Hour, Abner showed us where he's buried. Alcott really did kill him to keep the land," I said.

"Yes," Mrs. Whitney said. "So Abner's spirit stays at Creek Church waiting to be found."

I got up and stood in front of Mrs. Whitney. "But if we can retrieve his bones, can he leave that place?"

"Maybe," Mrs. Whitney said. "What we really need is an imprint of his beloved Sophie. He needs to feel her essence to know it's time to leave."

I thought of Mrs. Greene's attic. I was certain all of Sophie's belongings were locked up in that trunk.

If we had Sophie's things, we could convince him to leave Creek Church, and we could save him.

"I know how to get Sophie's belongings," I said.

"Your grandma still wants nothing to do with this," Mrs. Whitney said. "Nothing has changed."

"Don't worry," I said. "I think I know what we need to do."

I found everyone waiting for me at the picnic table in the yard.

"Where did you go?" Ellis asked. "We thought a haint kidnapped you!"

"I was getting worried," Jasper said. "Your mama will be here any minute now."

"I can't believe you didn't wake me up," Janie complained.

Dark circles appeared under their eyes, and I touched my own face for puffiness. I told them everything. How Mrs. Whitney had tried to save Abner's spirit before with Mrs. Greene. "Mrs. Whitney wants to dig up the grave," I said. "She agreed to help us."

"What's her plan?" Jasper asked.

"Her fiancé, Mr. Coolidge, is a mortician, just like Granddaddy Greene was. He knows people who can help us dig up Abner's grave," I said.

"It may not be that easy," Jasper said. "We couldn't get Abner to leave last night, and then you got those other haints. They might get even angrier if we take Abner away."

"Mrs. Whitney mentioned that," I said. "She says if we get some of Sophie's things, she believes it may convince him to leave."

"How you gonna get those things?" Ellis asked. "Ain't they locked up in Mrs. Greene's attic?"

They stared at me. I had told Mrs. Whitney it wouldn't be a problem, but I knew it would be a challenge.

"We have to get into the house without her knowing," I said.

"You can count me out," Ellis said. "Nope. Not interested."

Jasper looked at me as if I were crazy. "How will you get inside your grandma's house?"

Spending summers at Mrs. Greene's house had given me a bit of insider information: I knew where she kept her special things.

"She has a spare key, and I know where she hides it," I said. "We can go in while she's at the Deaconess Board meeting. She has one every Monday. Then we can help Abner for real."

"Do you have a death wish?" Ellis asked.

"I'm sorry," Jasper said. "This sounds all kinds of wrong."

"This is a solid plan," Janie said. "We don't need either of you."

Mama drove up to the trailer, and that was the end of our conversation. We gathered our things out of the tent and climbed into the car.

"You survived the wild outdoors." She smiled.

Ellis hopped in the front passenger seat and kissed her on her cheek. "I missed you, Mama."

"Oh, sweetheart," she said. "It was just one night."

"We could have died, though." Ellis sighed, and Janie kicked his seat.

Janie slid closer to me. "I like this new Sarah."

CHAPTER THIRTY-TWO
Hoodlum Children

On Monday morning I fried two eggs for Ellis and even made him pancakes. He focused on his food and wouldn't look at us.

"You sure you don't want to come with us?" Janie asked him.

"No," Ellis said. "I wanna keep my life."

"Nothing bad is gonna happen," I said. "Mrs. Greene will be at the Deaconess Board meeting. She's been going to that meeting since I've been on this earth."

"Fine. We don't need his help anyway," Janie said.

"It actually may be better if he doesn't go," I said. "We need bikes to get there."

"You can't take my bike!" Ellis protested.

"We'll be back before you know it," Janie said.

Ellis frowned but decided to just shove more pancakes into his mouth.

"Okay, we should leave," I said. "We need to have as much time as possible to find what we need."

Janie put on her backpack and watched me as I laced up my sneakers.

I felt her stare and looked up. "What?"

"Nothing." Janie smiled. "I just never thought you had it in you."

"What do you mean?"

"If you'd told me that you were down for breaking into our grandma's house to help a ghost boy, I would have thought that you were cuckoo. Yet here we are."

I stood up and walked to the doorway. "It's the right thing to do. We need to save Abner, even if that means breaking into Mrs. Greene's house. She'll thank us one day."

"Not a chance," Janie said.

We passed the den and found Ellis playing one of his video games. He dropped his console and crashed his car.

"Be careful, okay? At the first sign of trouble you need to bail out."

Janie and I went into the garage. My stomach was in knots. This wasn't my finest hour, and Mama would be disappointed, but I couldn't stand by and forget about Abner or the rest of the spirits trapped in Warrenville.

Janie rode ahead of me, gliding from side to side in the road. Most people in Warrenville had long been at work, so we didn't see any cars. After cruising on Hardeman Road and Westmore Trail, we rolled down the hill on Cherokee Road and then turned in to the driveway to Mrs. Greene's house. I looked at my watch. It was 11:13 a.m. with no car in sight. We rode along the side of the house to the backyard. If I remembered correctly, Mrs. Greene had hidden her spare key in a red plant pot.

We walked into the screened back porch. Janie tried the back doorknob. "Too bad country people lock their doors now. Where's the key?"

"She hid it in the sage last summer." I searched the row of plants. Thyme, oregano, and other herbs. My eyes locked on the red pot in the corner. "Found it," I said, and squatted down in front of it.

I put my finger in the pot and poked around, but all I felt were roots and grainy dirt between my fingers.

"Anything?" Janie asked.

I prodded deeper, and then my fingers hit against something hard. I kept digging. The key! I pulled it out of the dirt.

"There it is." Janie beamed at me.

We went to the back door. I eagerly put the key in the lock, but it wouldn't budge. "It's stuck," I said.

"Let me try." Janie took the key and wiped some more dirt off it before turning the key in the lock. Nothing.

"Maybe it's for the front door," I said.

Janie wiped the sweat off her forehead. "We can try."

We snuck to the front of the house. Same result.

"She changed the locks," I said. "Or this isn't the right key."

We scampered to the back again. We needed a new plan. There was a possibility Mrs. Greene had hidden another key somewhere else, but we didn't have enough time to look for it. We were wasting precious minutes.

"We should leave," I said. "We can't get in."

We walked farther into the backyard. Janie and I searched around the house until she pointed to an open upstairs window: Its curtains blew in the summer breeze.

"That's how we're getting in," she said.

"You're crazy."

"Do you want to get some of Sophie's stuff or not?" Janie asked.

"How are you going to get up there?"

Janie scanned the backyard and then headed to the shed near Mrs. Greene's garden. "She should have a ladder in here, right?"

"Isn't that kind of dangerous?"

"I'm not scared of heights," Janie said.

Janie opened the shed door and ventured inside. I held my nose to the smell of musty air and fertilizer. A rusty metal ladder leaned against the far wall.

"We can use this," Janie said.

I didn't like this idea at all. What if Janie fell off?

Janie brought the ladder out of the shed, and I got a dirty rag to remove the cobwebs and dead spiders. Then we pushed the ladder up against the house.

"You can hold it for me."

I swallowed hard and watched Janie climb up. When she got to the top, she swayed, and the ladder shifted to the left in my hands.

"Janie, be careful!"

"It's okay. Just a little higher than I thought."

She scooted onto the roof. I held my breath. If

Janie fell off the roof and broke her neck, Mama would kill me. Of course, breaking into Mrs. Greene's house would also get me killed, so I would be double dead.

Janie reached the window and climbed inside. After a few moments she leaned out and waved. "I'll meet you at the back porch."

It was weird being inside Mrs. Greene's house when she wasn't there. It smelled like her, but it was different because my grandma's force field wasn't present.

"Okay. We go to the attic, grab some of Sophie's stuff, and get out," Janie said.

"We need to move fast," I said. "We don't have much time."

We walked down the hallway and found Mrs. Greene's bedroom door wide open. I stopped in my tracks.

"What's wrong?" Janie asked.

Maybe Mrs. Greene had a keepsake in her bedroom. Surely she wouldn't lock away all of her mama's belongings in a trunk.

"Go ahead and get the stuff in the attic," I said. "I'm going to look in her room."

"Do you think that's a good idea?" Janie asked.

"Go ahead—I'll just take a quick look."

Janie trotted past me, opened the door to the attic, and disappeared up the stairs. I paused in the doorway of Mrs. Greene's bedroom. *Sorry, Grandma.* Her dresser gleamed in the sunlight, furniture-polish shiny. The sharp lemon scent filled my nostrils as I stepped over the doorsill. I stared at Granddaddy Greene's picture. He was in his Sunday best, a gentle smile on his face. I hoped he understood why I was doing this.

"Sorry, Granddaddy," I whispered.

I opened up the drawers and tentatively searched but found nothing. I swallowed hard when I looked underneath her socks and her underwear. I felt like a criminal.

After rummaging through the dresser and coming up empty, I inspected the closet. Nothing.

I was on my hands and knees, about to search under the bed, when I heard a car door slam. I bolted up and crept to the window. I peeked between the curtains, and my heart leaped out of my chest. Mrs. Greene's car was in the driveway! She had come back early from the Deaconess Board meeting! I rushed out of the bedroom to the attic.

"Janie! Mrs. Greene's back!"

My cousin appeared on the stairs. "I thought you said she wouldn't be here till noon?"

"I did, but she's here now!"

Janie rushed down the attic stairs. "Maybe we can sneak out."

"We can't sneak out! She's gonna find out the back door is unlocked! She's gonna find the ladder!" My breath came out in short bursts. This was a stupid, stupid idea. Janie held my hand, but it was useless. The end was near.

"Calm down," Janie said. "I don't need you to faint."

The front door opened with a jangle of keys, followed by Mrs. Greene singing some hymn. Maybe she would forgive with Jesus fresh in her heart, but I didn't have much faith in that thought right now.

"We're so dead," I said.

"Let's just wait it out in the attic," Janie replied.

Janie pulled me into the darkness and closed the attic door. We stood huddled at the bottom of the stairs.

"We need to leave," I whispered. "We can't stay here."

The muffled clang of pots and pans filtered up to us, signaling that Mrs. Greene was still in her kitchen.

Janie pulled out her phone, and a blue glow spread across her face. "I can't get a signal."

"Who are you trying to call?"

"Ellis. Maybe he can call her. Give us a distraction."

It was useless. Mrs. Greene was coming up the stairs. Her steps echoed in the hallway as Janie shoved her phone in her pocket and put her finger to her lips.

Mrs. Greene approached the attic door. Her shadow loomed in the light that seeped in beneath our feet. Janie grasped my hand so tight I knew it would leave a bruise. I held my breath. Mrs. Greene walked away.

Then we heard a scream.

Without thinking, I opened the attic door and ran down the hallway. Mrs. Greene was in her bedroom, standing in front of her open closet and dresser drawers. Her bosom rose up and down in heavy pants.

"Are you okay?" I asked.

She turned to us, and her eyes bulged in anger. "What are you doing in my house?!"

"We're surprise visiting you," Janie said. "Surprise!"

She grabbed us both by the crooks of our elbows and dragged us down the stairs. We tumbled after her.

"Don't you dare move," she said. Her voice was cold and lethal as she pushed us into the parlor. We fell to the floor like rag dolls.

I froze in place as if I had been injected with venom.

"Delilah?" she spat into the cordless phone. "You better get over here right now! I just found these hoodlum children in my house!"

CHAPTER THIRTY-THREE
Consequences

Janie and I sat in the parlor and stared at the two long switches on the table. Mrs. Greene had made us go out in the backyard to get them. Their fresh green smell filled me with fear.

Mrs. Greene had whipped me only once, when I was a little girl. I had been playing with the stove. Turning on all the burners, I watched the blue flames flicker and dance. I had been so mesmerized that I yelped when Mrs. Greene jerked me away. She tore into my legs with the switch she kept on top of the refrigerator. It took several days for the red welts to disappear. Mama had been furious, but Mrs. Greene insisted she had done it because she loved me.

Since that incident I had been afraid of getting in

trouble. I still remembered the pain of Mrs. Greene's wrath. So after that day I always did what Mrs. Greene told me.

Janie sat next to me with her arms crossed while Mrs. Greene sipped sweet tea and glared at us, her face flushed pink. My heart beat in rapid spurts.

I heard Mama's car in the driveway; her heels clicked in quick succession up the porch steps. She opened the front door and rushed into the parlor. She had on her blue suit with the yellow floral blouse she had bought at the Alton Mall.

"Delilah," Mrs. Greene said. "So nice you were able to leave the Fairfield County courthouse to manage the care of these children."

Mama glanced at us. I wanted to tell her everything, make her understand, even if she wouldn't believe me.

Mama looked wearily at Mrs. Greene. "Please just tell me what happened, Lena."

"I found these two in my house!" Mrs. Greene snapped. "Rambling upstairs."

"That doesn't seem right. How did they even get in?" Mama asked.

"They broke into my house." Mrs. Greene's face flushed a deeper pink; if steam could have come out of her ears, it would have been streaming out at this point. "Got a ladder from the shed and came through a window."

"Is this true?" Mama asked.

Mrs. Greene got up and stood in front of us. She pointed to the switches. "It took everything in me to wait until you got here. We need to take care of this. Right now."

Mama looked at the switches on the table. I wished more than ever that those switches were red velvet cake slices.

"I am *not* beating my children," she said.

"Why not?" Mrs. Greene asked. "This is what they need. It's certainly what they deserve. How are they going to learn?"

"We will discuss this like sane people," Mama said.

I sank farther into the couch. The disappointment grew on Mama's face. I couldn't even find the words to defend myself.

Finally her calm exterior shattered. "How could you have done this?!" she shouted at us. "Have you lost your mind? I don't care if this is your grandmother's house. You don't break into houses! I raised you better than this!"

So much for a sane conversation.

"It's not what you think," I started.

Mama interrupted me. "I don't want to hear any excuses."

Janie sprang up next to me on the couch. "It was my fault, Aunt Delilah. I made Sarah come here. It was all my idea."

"Janie, don't—it's okay," I said.

She put her hand on my leg and squeezed it tightly. "I've been so bored," Janie continued. "Sarah didn't want to come with me, but I finally convinced her. I wore her down."

Janie was standing up for me again.

"Is this true, Sarah?" Mama asked me.

"Sounds true enough to me," Mrs. Greene said. "They came into this house to meddle with my things. It was only a matter of time before Janie would ruin Sarah. Told you that child needed to be here with me."

"I'm sorry," Janie said. "I didn't mean any harm. This town is too small. There's nothing to do."

"Janie, this is unacceptable," Mama said.

Mrs. Greene's face was hard and focused. "What's unacceptable is you letting these children get away with all this." She picked up the switches. "I should have whipped you girls before she got here."

Mama closed her eyes and brought her hands to her temple. Counting to three wouldn't be enough to solve this problem.

"There will be nothing of that sort done today," Mama said firmly. "Robert is getting off work early so we can discuss this as a family."

Mrs. Greene held the switches tight in her hand and pointed them at us. "You do something like this again and not even Jesus will stop me from tearing into your hides. Delilah, get them out of my sight." She turned from us and went into the kitchen.

Mama shook her head and took a deep breath. "I'm so disappointed in you, Sarah."

Her words hurt so much worse than a switch ever would. I retreated deeper and deeper into myself.

"It was my fault, Aunt Delilah," Janie repeated with urgency.

"No more talking," Mama said.

"We should have told Mama the truth," I whispered as we drove away from Mrs. Greene's house.

"She won't believe us." Janie leaned into me. "Especially not in front of Mrs. Greene. We just have to find another way."

I shook my head. There was no other way. We

were in deep trouble. Who knew what Daddy would do when Mama told him the details? We should have just asked Mrs. Greene for Sophie's stuff, not broken into her house. *What was I thinking?* Maybe if we had just told her the truth and she knew that we had found out about Abner, she would have helped us. Instead we took the cowardly route of sneaking around. Now we would never know.

I watched Daddy pace the floor of Mama's office through the closed French doors. Mama sat at her desk. She was using her lawyerly hand gestures. I hoped she wasn't using words like "juvenile delinquents" and "criminal charges." Daddy finally stopped pacing and sat down in front of her. They huddled together; our fate was in their hands.

I sat on the couch between Ellis and Janie. Soiled napkins and paper plates littered the coffee table. Once again Daddy had come home with our supper in a box. Now I associated pizza with drama. I could take only a few tiny bites. My nerves were too wound up.

"Told y'all it was a stupid idea. I knew you would get caught." Ellis turned to Walter, who was resting on his shoulder. "Didn't I tell them?"

"Doesn't matter now." Janie scratched under Walter's neck, and he stuck out his tongue.

"We should have told them the truth," I said.

"They would have never believed us," Janie said.

Ellis grabbed another slice of pizza. "Y'all committed a felony. Might not go to jail but gonna be grounded for the rest of your life."

"You'll be grounded right along with us," Janie said.

Mama opened the French doors, and she and Daddy walked out and stood in front of us.

Daddy shook his head. "I don't even know where to start with all of you."

Janie shifted behind me and focused on her nails. She had scraped off most of the red polish. Ellis shoved the rest of his pizza into his mouth. I sat silent between them; my whole body was shaking.

"We can't let you stay at the house by yourselves any longer," Mama said.

"You gonna get us a babysitter?" Ellis asked.

Daddy and Mama exchanged glances. Panic rose up my chest and lodged in my throat. I knew what was coming.

"No babysitter. We're going back to the old summer routine," Daddy said. "You'll be staying at your grandma's house during the day."

Ellis stood up fast. "Why I got to be punished with them?"

Janie pulled him back down on the couch, and Walter crawled into her lap.

"So you didn't know anything about this?" Daddy asked him.

"I told them it was a bad idea." Ellis bowed his head. "Doesn't that count?"

"He was too scared to go so he gave me his bike," Janie said.

"I wasn't scared!" Ellis protested.

"Be quiet," I told him. "You're only making it worse."

Mama tightened the sash on her robe. "You'll be grounded for the rest of the summer. When you're not at your grandmother's house, you'll be up in your rooms. No TV. No playing outside. No walking to Town Square. Jasper and Jovita won't be able to visit."

"You won't need to worry about Jovita," Janie mumbled.

"Young lady!" Mama used her loud lawyer voice. "I'm the only one who should be talking here."

My cousin receded into the couch and remained silent.

"Your privileges will also be taken away," Mama continued. "Ellis, that means no video games. Janie, no Internet for your phone. Sarah, no science symposium."

Her words sounded far away, muted and slow, as if Mama spoke to me from another dimension.

"Why can't you take her space books away instead?" Janie asked. "I told you it was my fault."

"These are the consequences for her actions," Daddy said.

All my limbs felt heavy. Now I wouldn't be able to go to the science symposium. I wouldn't be able to hear the latest news on the planets or moons. Newly formed tears stung my eyes.

The rest of the summer would pass like dog years. Mrs. Greene would work us to the bone. The promise of the switch would hang over our heads. But unlike today, I believed Mama would give Mrs. Greene permission to whip our hides.

"Now, we don't want to be blindsided with any more foolery. So this is your last chance. Is there anything else we should know about?"

Mama looked at each of us. This was the time to tell them. Everything. Creek Church. The cameo. The boy. The message. The protective salt and pouches.

The Witching Hour. The haints. This was the time to let my parents know we were only trying to do the right thing. We were only trying to save our family. Save our town.

"Sarah?" Daddy squatted down in front of me. "Do you have something to say?"

Janie and Ellis both looked at me. They didn't want me to tell the truth. They didn't think Mama and Daddy would believe us.

I swallowed. "We're sorry."

CHAPTER THIRTY-FOUR
Worst Fears

The next morning we got into Mama's car. Every once in a while Mama looked in the rearview mirror at me, the disappointment still fresh on her face. I had broken my promise to handle my responsibility this summer. I had failed. I avoided her glances and focused on the pastures and cows we passed along the road.

Mama pulled into Mrs. Greene's driveway and then turned to face us. "I'm no longer mad at you. We all make mistakes. I just hope you've learned your lesson so this doesn't happen again."

"You don't have to worry about me," Ellis said. "But I can't vouch for these two."

Janie sneered at him and opened the car door. Ellis

and I followed her outside, but Mama didn't budge.

"Aunt Delilah, you're not getting out?" Janie asked.

"You can't blame her," Ellis said.

"I need to get to court. Go ahead." Mama motioned for us to hurry up.

We walked up the steps to the house. Exotic plants stood behind thick glass and taunted birds to fly into the mirage, dazed and confused. Too bad we couldn't be those birds today and fly in the other direction. We opened the front door and found Mrs. Greene in the kitchen, washing dishes. She had on a dusty shirt and faded overalls. When she heard us, she turned around—then frowned.

"Why did Delilah let you wear your street clothes over here?" She pulled off her rubber gloves. "This is not gonna work."

Mrs. Greene went upstairs and found three old Heritage Festival T-shirts. We took turns going into the hall bathroom to put them on. They were huge and fell to the top of our knees. I adjusted the straps of my training bra. The T-shirts smelled of bleach and felt crunchy, as if they had dried out in the sun.

After putting on our summer work uniform, our grandma then slathered sunscreen on our faces, arms,

281

and legs. She gave Janie and me straw hats but gave Ellis a baseball cap that had belonged to Granddaddy Greene. She inspected each of us before she pushed us outside.

Mrs. Greene followed behind us with a metal folding chair she got from the back porch and placed it in the shade of a sycamore tree.

"I need y'all to go through my corn and see what's good for picking. I promised Sister Benton I would have something for her at tomorrow's Bible study." She sat and crossed her legs as we stood in front of her in the blazing sun. "Go on now. I don't have all day."

We meandered through the rows of tall green stalks. Janie was having a hard time figuring out which corn ears were ready.

"Don't get that one. The silk is still green," I said.

"Watch out for the worms," Ellis added.

Janie jerked her hand away. "I hate corn."

"Hold the basket," I told her. "I'll pick out the ears."

Ellis wiped away his sweat mustache. "Just like old times, right, Sarah?"

I walked farther down the row and picked out two ears of corn and put them in Janie's basket. This wasn't like old times. Even though it was wrong to break into Mrs. Greene's house, we had done it to help someone. But nobody knew that. Abner still needed our help, and now we were out here picking corn as punishment instead of doing something.

We gathered up a basketful of corn and delivered it to the back porch. Mrs. Greene got up and put a long sheet of plastic on the cement floor.

"Dump that basket here," she said. "I need you to shuck all this corn. When you're done with that, you can move on to snapping and shelling the peas." She pointed to two overflowing metal bins.

"Can I use the bathroom?" Janie asked.

Mrs. Greene frowned. "Don't take too long, and you better be right back. Don't try nothing slick, either."

Janie bowed her head. "Yes, ma'am."

Ellis and I sat on the floor on top of the plastic and started shucking the corn. I removed the silk worms, and Ellis broke the sheath of each ear with a hard snap.

"She's gonna work us until we ain't got no sense left," Ellis said.

"It could be worse," I replied.

"Don't jinx it," Ellis said. "Day ain't over yet."

Janie appeared on the back porch. She sighed as she sat in front of us.

"You need to start shelling the peas," I said.

She pushed the metal bin across the concrete floor with her feet. "Don't worry. We're going to be okay."

"Don't feel like it," Ellis grumbled. "If I get heat stroke and die today, I'm gonna put a curse on both of you."

"Don't talk about curses," I snipped.

As soon as we were done, Mrs. Greene gave us our next chore of digging and clearing out old plants and preparing rows for okra, bell peppers, and cucumbers. The sun beat down on my shoulders, and when I rubbed my eyes, I saw black spots. The heat was relentless, and with no breeze, my T-shirt was soaked with sweat. Mrs. Greene was cramming a whole summer list of chores into one day.

"Take them shirts off and put your street clothes back on," Mrs. Greene said when we were finished. "I can't let you sit at my table looking a hot mess."

We took turns in the hall bathroom to freshen up before we sat at the kitchen table. Ellis stared at a wrapped iced Bundt cake. I hoped he had the sense not to ask for a slice. Without a doubt, I knew that cake wasn't meant for us. We wouldn't be having any of our grandma's cakes anytime soon.

I grabbed the pitcher on the table and poured a glass; the liquid coated my tongue with the taste of extra-bitter leaves, and I almost spit it back up. "This is unsweet tea."

Mrs. Greene narrowed her eyes at me. "Not wasting my sugar on ungrateful, meddling children."

I knew better than to argue and stayed quiet. I was about to take another sip—I was that thirsty—when I heard a car in the driveway. Mrs. Greene got up from the table and went out on the front porch.

Janie smiled at us. "We got company."

We sneaked through the parlor and stood behind the glass front door to see who was coming to visit. A long black car was in the driveway. The windows were tinted dark, but Mr. Coolidge was already walking around to the passenger side. When he opened the door, his fiancée stepped out of the car.

Mrs. Whitney took his hand, and they stopped at the bottom of the steps.

Mrs. Greene stood her ground on the porch with her arms crossed, a scowl on her face.

"Why are you here at my house?"

CHAPTER THIRTY-FIVE
Change of Heart

Mr. Coolidge looked ready to attend a funeral, with his dark suit and hat, but I guessed since he was a mortician, he needed to be ready at all times. Mrs. Whitney was in a different long white dress, and she wore her usual three necklaces. Janie and Ellis came up behind me and peered out onto the porch.

"I told you we would be okay," Janie said.

I turned to her. "You knew they were coming?"

"I saved the number to the Train Depot on my phone, so I called her when I went to the bathroom earlier." She pulled her phone out from her shorts pocket.

I widened my eyes. "Did you take your phone back from Mama's drawer?"

Ellis shook his head. "You can't value your life."

Janie shrugged. "We need to help Abner. Not be farmhands all summer."

I smiled at my cousin as we turned and looked back at the drama unfolding outside. Mrs. Whitney stood at the bottom of the steps. She touched the large black stone of her longest necklace before she spoke.

"We need to talk, Lena," she said.

"Do we?" Mrs. Greene put her hands on her hips. Even in faded overalls, she carried herself as if she was wearing an evening gown. "I don't appreciate you coming to my house uninvited."

"But I was invited. Your granddaughter called me," Mrs. Whitney replied. "She said you were ready to talk."

Mrs. Greene turned and saw us at the front door. "I can guess which one did that."

Mr. Coolidge took off his hat and grappled with it in his hands. "Maybe we should go inside?"

Mrs. Greene laughed. "Now, Sylvester, you should know better than that. Nobody comes into my house unless I say so."

Mrs. Whitney shook her head. "Still stubborn as ever."

"You didn't answer my question," Mrs. Greene said. "Why are you at my house?"

"Lena, the children know," Mrs. Whitney said.

"Know what?"

"They know about Abner."

Mrs. Greene's hands fell off her hips and lay limp at her sides. At first she looked confused, but then her face flushed pink, and she balled her hands up into fists. "How did they find out? Did you tell them?" Her voice came out in angry waves.

"I didn't tell them anything," Mrs. Whitney said. "They saw the boy at Creek Church, and they came to me with questions."

Mrs. Greene turned back around and glared at us. "What did I tell you about going down there to that place?"

Ellis cowered behind me. Janie clasped my hand and squeezed it tight.

"Not too many folks have seen that boy," Mrs. Whitney said. "But these children saw him."

"Abner is long dead," Mrs. Greene said. "He's in the hands of the Lord."

"He's not. And you know that. Do you want to leave him with spirits who will eat at his soul? Those evil spirits are tricking Abner," Mrs. Whitney said. "They covet his light and keep him trapped. They will keep taking from him until there is nothing left. Then Abner will succumb to that same evil."

"You should know all about that," Mrs. Greene huffed. "You don't even respect the Lord. You come back to town with your witch roots and try to desecrate my grandchildren."

Janie opened the glass door and stepped out on the porch. She moved too fast for me to stop her. Ellis and I glanced at each other and quickly followed her.

"Mrs. Whitney was only trying to help us," Janie said. "When we saw the ghost boy in the picture and read Sophie's diary—"

Mrs. Greene grabbed Janie's arm. "I knew you were the cause of all this trouble. Always meddling in grown folks business."

Janie tried to step away from her. "You're hurting me."

"Wait—" I said.

"Lena, let that child go," Mr. Coolidge said.

"This is my house!" she shouted. "You have no right telling me what to do. Spreading these lies to my grandchildren. Disrespecting my wishes. I told you I was done with all of it!"

Mrs. Greene's wrath was spewing from her mouth, her eyes hard and cold. She took Janie into the house. I knew exactly where she was going.

I couldn't let Janie take the brunt of Mrs. Greene's punishment. I ran into the house after them. Mrs. Greene was in the kitchen and had reached up to the refrigerator to get one of the switches. Her face was twisted with anger, the long thick switch firm in her grasp. Janie was on the floor crying. I stood over her in a protective stance.

"Move, Sarah." Mrs. Greene's voice shook.

"No," I said.

"Move!" Mrs. Greene shouted.

"No!" I shouted back.

My knees trembled in fear, but I stood my ground. "You need to listen to us! We're not lying! We saw Abner with our own eyes!" I cried out.

Mrs. Greene stood in complete shock in front of me. Mrs. Whitney and Mr. Coolidge had come into the house with Ellis. My brother's chest heaved up and down, his face stunned with fear.

"You don't know what you're talking about," Mrs. Greene said.

"It's true," I said. "We saw Abner. I didn't want to believe it at first. Like you, I thought it didn't make any logical sense and we should forget about it. But then he came to our house and tried to communicate with us. When we went back to Creek Church, he showed us what had happened. Evern . . . killed him. Abner showed us where he's buried."

Mrs. Greene's eyes filled with tears.

"Abner needs our help. Please, help us. Please." I took her trembling hand. "We're the only ones that can do it. He's been waiting all these years for someone to save him so he can rest in peace. So he can finally be with Sophie. With your mama."

Janie stood up and wiped her eyes, Ellis now beside her. Together they placed their hands on top of ours. Mrs. Greene's face crumpled, and she began to cry.

"I knew Evern had something to do with it. When I was a little girl, I used to see him in town." Mrs. Greene's voice cracked with emotion. "No justice. The best day of my life was when he died. I know he's burning in hell for what he did."

"Wasn't too much we could do about Evern Alcott in those days," Mr. Coolidge said.

"But it's not like that anymore," Janie said. "Things have changed."

"Have they?" Mrs. Greene sniffed. "The only change I've seen is that men like Evern Alcott don't wear white sheets anymore. Some things haven't changed at all."

"But Warrenville has changed," I said. "From when you were young? To now? You can't deny that truth."

Mrs. Whitney moved closer and touched Mrs. Greene's shoulder. "Lena, we're not going backward. We'll never go back there. We're going to press forward whether they like it or not. And we'll always remember. This is why we need to set things right, first with Abner, and then with the rest of the spirits haunting Creek Church. There are other places around town with haints, too. Heal this town once and for all."

Mrs. Greene nodded and wiped her eyes. She pulled Janie in close to her. "I'm sorry, baby. I'm so sorry. I—" She faltered, too caught up in emotion.

Janie wiped tears from her face. "I'm sorry too."

Mr. Coolidge straightened his suit and placed his hat snugly on his head. "Let's go help this boy."

CHAPTER THIRTY-SIX

Love and Faith

Mrs. Greene and Mrs. Whitney rambled around the house, collecting items. Janie, Ellis, and I sat in the parlor, afraid to get in the way. It was as if we were in a dream that might disappear at any moment in the afternoon sunlight.

Mrs. Greene carried a glossy box, and she placed it on the table.

"What's in there?" Ellis asked.

"Some of Sophie's things from the attic," Mrs. Whitney said.

She opened the box to reveal a few of the items Janie and I had seen in the locked trunk. The delicately worn cotton-and-lace dress, the picture of Sophie and Abner, and the diary.

Mrs. Whitney took off her necklace with the black stone and placed it inside. "I have blessed this hematite with a spell to remove obstacles from our path and guard us from harm."

"Harm?" Ellis jerked his body upright.

"You must understand these spirits don't want Abner to leave," Mrs. Whitney said as she guided us to the car.

"Wait," Ellis said.

"Don't tell me you're still being a scaredy-cat?" Janie rolled her eyes.

"Ellis, what's wrong?" I asked.

He lowered his head, suddenly shy. "We've been through a lot this summer."

Janie raised her eyebrows. "And?"

"What about Jasper?" Ellis stared at his feet. "He won't be with us."

"That Johnson boy? From the trailer park?" Mrs. Greene asked.

"He works for me," Mrs. Whitney said. "A fine young man."

"He helped us discover where Abner is buried," I said.

"Then I guess we should go fetch him," Mrs. Greene said.

• • •

When we arrived at Jasper's trailer, he was dumping water into one of the birdbaths. Mrs. Greene rolled down her window and smiled. "Jasper Johnson, how are you doing today?"

Jasper dropped his bucket. This was the first time Mrs. Greene had spoken to him in a nice manner, and it had caught him off guard.

Ellis opened the car door. "We tried to call you, but no one answered the phone."

Jasper blinked. "What's going on?"

Janie pushed Ellis out of the way. "We're getting Abner out."

Jasper widened his eyes. "Right now?"

"Yes," Janie said. "Get in."

We squeezed in to make room for him in the backseat. Mrs. Greene didn't say anything about Jasper's dirty sneakers.

"Ellis insisted we come get you," I said.

Jasper gave Ellis a high five. "Good looking out."

When we arrived at Creek Church, Mrs. Greene parked behind Mr. Coolidge's sleek black car. He was with his sons, who were also morticians. In front of Mr. Coolidge's car was a truck, and two men in overalls were leaning on the hood. The truck held all sorts of shovels and a wheelbarrow. I knew at once they were the gravediggers.

"Y'all all right?" Mr. Coolidge asked them.

The men pointed to the woods behind the church foundation. Shadows shifted through the branches.

"We didn't come here to mess with no haints, sir," one of them said.

Mrs. Whitney laughed. "Grown men afraid of what these four children have faced. You should be ashamed. Where is your faith?"

The men remained silent. I grabbed Janie's hand, and she reached for Ellis's, who then grabbed on to Jasper: a human chain.

We walked toward the church steps.

Streaks of sunlight came through the green darkness. Whispers surrounded us and vibrated in my chest as the wind whipped through the air. When we arrived at the graveyard, warm puffs escaped my mouth, and I began to shiver.

Mrs. Greene and Mrs. Whitney walked through the tall weeds and grass to stare at the giant oak.

"Same as before," Mrs. Greene said. "Still dead."

"You know about the black tree?" I asked.

"This is where a lot of the victims were killed," Mrs. Whitney said.

"God bless their souls." Mr. Coolidge pressed his Bible to his chest.

The mist in the trees grew heavy, and I was beginning to get nervous. We still hadn't seen Abner. The sunlight no longer penetrated the growing mist. The woods grew darker.

"There, I see it." I pointed at the rocks. Daphnis was still where I had left her.

Mr. Coolidge motioned the gravediggers to come forth with their equipment. One of them opened a bag full of shovels while the other moved the rocks.

The wind strengthened; faint whispers lingered in the air like white noise. I wondered if the others heard them.

"So much evil," Mrs. Whitney said.

"Now she notices," Ellis mumbled.

The air grew icy as the whispers heightened. The gravediggers' shovels trembled. When they broke ground, a thunderous roar erupted around us. I clasped my hands over my ears to block out the terrifying sound. The gravediggers dropped their shovels and ran toward the road.

"Come back!" Janie shouted.

Jasper and Ellis moved closer to us. We huddled against the strong winds and wicked noises.

"I command you to let us take this child in the name of Sophie's love and faith!" Mrs. Whitney raised her voice as she clutched the box with Sophie's belongings. The deep roar turned into malicious laughter. The wind strengthened with bone-chilling gusts. Mrs. Greene had to hold Mrs. Whitney up against the force.

Mrs. Whitney and Mrs. Greene now held the box together in their arms. They looked frail against the strong wind. Mr. Coolidge stayed in front of Abner's unmarked grave and held up his Bible.

"We have to get the diary," I told Janie. "It may be the only way."

Janie and I struggled against the force of the wind. I grabbed Mrs. Whitney's hand. "Open the box!" I yelled.

Janie retrieved the diary and raised it above her head. I grabbed her arm to keep the book from flying out of her hands.

"Abner!" Janie shouted.

Mr. Coolidge quickly put his Bible between his knees, picked up a shovel, and started to dig.

"We need to help dig," Jasper said to us. "Grab a shovel."

Ellis and I picked up shovels, and Mrs. Greene supported Janie against the wind.

The earth moved under our efforts, and the sharp smell of freshly turned dirt filled our noses. The weight of the shovel strained my arms. Despite the pain and the wind, we weren't giving up.

"I hit something!" I said.

Mr. Coolidge bent down and began to move the dirt away from my shovel. A dull white bone revealed itself, and the wind instantly weakened, as if we had pulled a lever to release something.

The mist shifted, lifting up into the sky; sunlight filtered through the trees. We were in a completely different setting. Bright yellow light danced around us, casting the leaves as shadows on the red Georgia clay.

"These are a child's bones," Mr. Coolidge said.

Jasper stood up from the grave and examined the woods. I followed his gaze to see a dark shadow spin through the foliage before it broke apart and floated toward our group. We stood silent, afraid to move. Before our eyes the shadow transformed into a human shape.

The woods twinkled and revealed Abner's translucent form. He moved closer to the open grave and touched the red clay. A bright shimmer rose up, and rays of light swirled and bounced around him.

"Amazing grace." Mr. Coolidge touched his Bible.

The light welcomed Abner, but he stayed where he was, enthralled like everyone else.

"What is he waiting for?" Ellis asked.

"I don't know," Jasper whispered back.

Taking the diary from Janie, I placed it at Abner's feet. "It's time for you to go home, Abner. Sophie is waiting for you."

Abner turned to look at me, his face alight with pure joy. He slowly walked into the light, dissolving into the prism of radiance. And was gone.

Mrs. Whitney placed the lid on the box. "He's finally at peace."

I stared at Sophie's diary on the ground. I picked it up and held the book close to me.

The branches of the black tree seemed to come alive and snapped to attention. Green leaves sprouted out, and the black bark turned a warm brown. The wind sighed through branches as the sun bathed the tree in light.

Heavy footsteps rushed through the woods. One of Mr. Coolidge's sons appeared.

"Sir, we have a problem," he said. "Folks are here

wanting to know what's going on. We've tried to hold them back, but there are too many."

"The gravediggers snitched on us." Janie frowned.

"It's okay. We've done what we needed to do." Mrs. Greene wiped the tears from her eyes. "Come, children."

"What about Abner's bones?" Janie asked.

"We will take care of them," Mr. Coolidge said.

Ellis pulled Janie away from the grave, and we walked back toward the road. Word had traveled fast. Sunnie and Mrs. Loren were there. So were Mr. Hawkins and Ms. Bell the librarian. Even the women of the Deaconess Board strained to get a better look. Grown folks in aprons, hard hats, and uniforms. Mr. Coolidge's sons were holding most of them back. In the front of the crowd, my parents struggled to get through.

"Uh-oh. How did they find out?" Janie asked.

"Mama's going to kill us," Ellis mumbled.

Daddy broke through the crowd with Mama. "What is going on? What are y'all doing here?"

"I took the children to your house for them to be safe!" Mama shouted at Mrs. Greene. "Not to come to Creek Church for some craziness!"

Mrs. Greene smiled at Mama. "Calm down, Delilah. The children are fine. No harm done."

She moved toward us in the speed only mamas have.

Daddy held her back. "They do look all right." He had lost some of the formality in his voice. "What were y'all doing back in the woods?"

"We had to help our blood kin," Mrs. Greene said.

Mama smoothed out her wrinkled suit and whispered to Daddy. He let go of his grasp. She moved up the stone steps.

"Sarah, are you all right?" she asked me.

"Yes, I'm fine," I said.

She touched Janie's arm. "Janie, how about you?"

"Mama, what about me?" my brother whined. "You didn't ask me."

"Ellis," Mama sighed. "Are you okay?"

"I'm hungry." He rubbed his stomach, and Jasper laughed.

Mrs. Greene patted Mama on her back. "Delilah, I can't believe they let you out of the Fairfield County courthouse because of some nonsense on Linnard Run."

"These are my children!" Mama cried.

"Okay, let's go." Daddy gathered us and snagged Jasper, who was about to join Mr. Coolidge's sons. "You too."

"Are we going somewhere to eat?" Ellis asked.

"No," Mama and Daddy replied in unison.

"I will never understand your grandmother," Mama mumbled as we got in the car.

I turned and looked out the car window. Mrs. Greene and Mrs. Whitney stood on the church steps. They both held Sophie's box and peered into the crowd. All the years had melted away, and they were friends again. Mr. Coolidge came back through the woods. He held his Bible and kissed Mrs. Whitney on the cheek. Even from our distance, I could hear her laughter through the thick glass.

CHAPTER THIRTY-SEVEN
Home

After that day, Mrs. Whitney and Mrs. Greene helped other Warrenville families with their spiritual problems. Together they guided the town's blood kin to release the haints so they could finally rest in peace. Mr. Coolidge took care of Abner's bones, and everyone came together and raised money to buy a tombstone for the Greene burial plot in Evergreen Cemetery.

The townsfolk eventually held a memorial service for all the victims of Warrenville's violent past. Pastor Munroe gave a eulogy, and Mrs. Whitney unveiled her plans for erecting a Wall of Remembrance in Marigold Park. Family members spoke the names of the spirits they had helped, and I stated

Abner's name into the wind. After so many years, he was finally with Sophie and the rest of our family. At the end of the service, the ladies of the Deaconess Board released white doves into the summer sky.

Aunt Gina finished filming her movie in Paris and returned to Warrenville with a suitcase filled with gifts for Janie, who squealed with delight. She had finally been reunited with her mama. Now they were planning to move to California, and Janie's Hollywood dreams were coming true.

On Janie and Aunt Gina's last night in Warrenville, Mrs. Greene hosted a celebration supper at her house. Janie and I sat next to Mrs. Whitney and Mr. Coolidge while we waited for Ellis to say the grace.

"Try not to go overboard," Daddy said.

Ellis nodded and bowed his head. "Lord? Let this food nourish our bodies, minds, and hearts. Amen."

"That's the shortest prayer you've said all summer," Janie laughed.

We piled up our plates, and only the sounds of happy murmurs and the clicking of forks filled the room. Afterward, Mrs. Greene served her county-famous red velvet cake. No doubt she had baked it especially for us.

"This cake is like a slice of home," Aunt Gina said.

"Warrenville will always be your home," Mrs. Greene said. "No matter how fancy and famous you get."

As the celebration continued, a deep, joyful warmth spread through me. Mr. Coolidge fed Mrs. Whitney a forkful of cake. Mama nodded as she listened intently to Aunt Gina describe her trip to the Palace of Versailles. Mrs. Greene beamed as she gave Ellis another thick slice of her red velvet cake. Daddy caught my eye and grinned at me from across the table. I think he felt the same happiness too.

Janie touched my shoulder. "Do you want to help me pack up the rest of my stuff?"

I followed Janie upstairs to Aunt Gina's room. All of her things had already been packed, so I was confused. She opened up her pink backpack and pulled out the silver hand that she had taken from the gift shop.

"Can you give this back to Mrs. Whitney? Tell her I'm sorry?"

I took the silver hand from her. "I already knew you had it."

"Why didn't you say anything?"

"I didn't want you to know that I was snooping

in your things," I said. "So sorry about that. I was wrong."

"I was wrong too. I don't have the right to take things that don't belong to me. I know that now," she said with a shy smile.

I put the silver hand in my pocket. "I'm sure Mrs. Whitney will accept your apology now that you're giving it back."

Janie grinned. "Thanks."

She opened up her suitcase and took out one of her Paris gifts, a heavy snow globe of delicate silver stars with a crescent moon in its center. I remembered gasping when Aunt Gina had given it to Janie.

"I want you to have this," she said.

"Janie," I whispered. "I can't take this."

She pushed it into my hands. "You don't have a choice."

Shaking the globe, I watched the stars float and settle like snowfall.

"I know how crazy you are about moons." Janie smiled at me as she zipped up her suitcase. "I hope you have fun at the science symposium. Try not to be a nag and ask too many questions," she said with a laugh.

Even though I was still technically on punishment, somehow Mrs. Greene had convinced my parents to let me go to the science symposium next month. I don't know what she told them, but whatever it was, it had worked.

"You know I already have tons of questions, so I can't promise anything," I said, a lump suddenly forming in my throat. "I'm really going to miss you."

"We'll stay in touch," Janie said. "We just have to convince Aunt Delilah to get you a phone."

"It won't be the same. I won't have anyone here to talk to."

"You have Jovita," she said.

"I thought you didn't like her," I replied.

Janie shrugged. "I think you should give her another chance."

I remembered how Jovita had hugged me tight during the memorial service at Marigold Park. She was truly sorry. If Mrs. Greene and Mrs. Whitney could rekindle their friendship, at least I could try with Jovita.

"What are you two doing in here?" Ellis appeared in the doorway with Jasper.

"I came over to say good-bye," Jasper said.

"That's nice." Janie gave both of them a suitcase. "You can take these out to the car."

We followed the boys downstairs and joined

everyone on the porch. Daddy put the suitcases in the trunk for their trip to the Atlanta airport. Janie and Aunt Gina had to go back to Chicago so they could get all of their belongings. Then they would drive out west to California and start a new life.

Everyone hugged Janie and Aunt Gina. Mrs. Greene wiped away her tears. Mama smoothed out my cousin's braids and told her to take care of her mama. Mrs. Whitney kissed Janie on the forehead and uttered a small blessing; then she gave her a necklace with a green stone.

Janie and I walked down the porch steps, our hands intertwined. The lump in my throat returned, and I blinked back tears.

"I'll miss you, too." Janie gave me one last hug. "You'll have to come visit me in California."

"Next summer," I whispered in her ear. "You can show me all the mansions and movie stars."

Ellis grumbled behind us. "We ain't got time for all this emotional stuff. You gonna make her miss her flight."

"Oh, I'll miss you, Ellis." Janie grabbed my brother, and he squirmed, trying to escape our clutches. We pulled him tighter into our hug and showered him with kisses.

Janie and Aunt Gina waved good-bye as Daddy drove them away. It was a bittersweet end to the summer, but I knew no matter how far we traveled in this universe, this place of shared roots would always be home.

ACKNOWLEDGMENTS

Bringing a book into the world can be overwhelming but I was lucky to have many people help make this dream come true.

Forever grateful to Beth Phelan, the creator of #DVpit. Who knew my road to publication would begin with a tweet? Beth, I love how you put action behind your words and you should be so proud of the books that have been published because of your passion.

To my agent, Victoria Marini, I'm so thankful for your belief in me. From the beginning, you saw my potential and had the confidence that I was capable of revising this story into its best form. I appreciate all of your support.

Thank you to the Simon & Schuster BFYR team and everyone who helped turn my story into a real, physical book. To my acquiring editor, Mekisha Telfer, who was the first champion of my story and for my editor Krista Vitola, who led me down the path to a deeper story and helped give this story a stronger heartbeat.

One of the best things about my journey to publication is meeting the other writers who I've come to know and cherish. Hugs and kisses to my Team Marini crew: Dhonielle Clayton, Sona Charaipotra, Claire Legrand, Bethany

C. Morrow, Hanna Alkaf, Margaret Owen, Anna Meriano, Elsie Chapman, Zoraida Córdova, and Ida Olson.

So much love to the writer friends who gave me support and advice: Roselle Lim, Meredith Ireland, Isabel Sterling, Jennifer Dugan, Nafiza Azad, Aminah Mae Safi, Patrice Caldwell, Samira Ahmed, Sandhya Menon, Gloria Chao, Karuna Riazi, Olugbenmisola Rhuday-Perkovich, Kelly Starling Lyons, Linda Williams Jackson, Lisa Moore Ramée, Natasha Diaz, Rebecca Barrow, Mark Oshiro, Kat Cho, Claribel Ortega, Kosòko Jackson, Justin A. Reynolds, S.A. Chakraborty, J. Zeynab Joukhadar, Laura Pohl, Ryan La Sala, Nicole Melleby, Nova Ren Suma, Julie C. Dao, Yamile Mendez, Nic Stone, Angie Thomas, Heather McCorkle, Julie Falatko, Tamara Ireland Stone, Justine Larbalestier, Karen M. McManus, Heidi Heilig, Janae Marks, Paula Chase, Vicky Alvear Shecter, Elisbeth Norton, and Phalia McCorckle-Kester.

For my first writing mentor, Carol Lee Lorenzo, who ignited the spark for this book with a writing exercise at the Callonwolde Arts Center.

To my mother, who taught me that anything is possible with focus and dedication. Your passion for public libraries and books were the reasons I fell in love with words. I hope that you're proud of me.

To my father, who told me that being smart was an

asset and not a liability. You led me into the fascinating world of science and technology. I miss you every day, but I know you're still rooting for me and will always remain my biggest fan.

A Reading Group Guide to

Just
South
of
Home

by Karen Strong

About the Book

Sarah and her younger brother, Ellis, along with their cousin Janie and Ellis's friend Jasper, decide to investigate the hauntings at the old Creek Church. After carelessly awakening restless spirits that cause strange and otherworldly occurrences, the group has no idea how to lead these earthbound souls to rest. Motivated by compassion and a determination to bring peace to one of their own kin, the children discover the power of conviction and the belief in a purpose much greater than themselves. With the help of an eccentric local woman and a young boy from a very different time, this brave group finds the courage to heal a small southern town haunted by a dark history of racial injustice. As the people of Warrenville eventually bear witness to the fear and hatred that provoked unspeakable past cruelties, their respect, love, and hope allow other spirits to fully cross over and finally rest in peace. *Just South of Home* is more than a ghost story; it challenges readers to look at the fear found at the core of racially motivated hatred and violence, to recognize conflicting ideas, and to speak out against prejudice in order to shape a better future.

Discussion Questions

1. Can you predict any of the story's plot from the cover? What did it suggest to you, or what kinds of emotions did it evoke? Did it make you want to read the book?

2. Sarah's first-person narrative creates the story's tone. Can you relate to her voice? How might the story have differed if it were told from another character's point of view?

3. Describe the community of Warrenville. How does its dark history contribute to the unfolding story? How does the community react?

4. At the beginning of the novel, Sarah is a cautious, mature, and responsible small-town girl living "inside her head" while Janie is the adventurous city girl governed by her own rules and risk-taking impulses. It's in Janie's nature "to want to explore and get into trouble." What do the cousins learn from each other by the end of the story? What do they learn about themselves?

5. Why don't the children tell an adult about the strange happenings? Do you agree or disagree with this choice? What would you have done under those circumstances? Explain your answers. What are the consequences for Sarah and her friends?

6. Ellis wants nothing to do with Sarah's and Janie's plans, but the girls insist they all explore Creek Church further. Describe Ellis's response. Do you think his fears are justified? Have you ever been asked to go along with something you didn't want to do? How did it make you feel?

7. What do you think about Janie's habit of stealing things? What is the difference between finding things and taking things? Is it ever right to take something that doesn't belong to you? What is the significance of the cameo Janie takes from the graveyard?

8. Mrs. Whitney tells Sarah and Janie, "'Haints are trapped. This earthly plane is not their home anymore. They will always seek refuge until they are released to their true place of belonging.'" What do the haints need in order to be released and finally rest in peace? What does it mean to belong?

9. Mrs. Whitney is isolated by her community, suffering prejudices over her beliefs and folk practices. Why do you think people are so quick to judge her? What do the items she sells in her gift shop reveal about her? Explain your answers.

10. Mrs. Whitney makes amulets for the children and their family members to wear for protection. What is an amulet? She also gives Sarah a talisman for her windowsill. What is the difference between an amulet and a talisman?

11. What does Mrs. Whitney mean when she says to Sarah, "'You can use whatever you like, child. Its power is in your belief'"? What do you think she means when she says, "'Money is just one form of energy, child'"? Do you think Sarah finds this advice helpful? Explain your answers.

12. The author presents many recognizable themes. Cite examples of peer pressure, bullying, snobbery, loneliness, loss, disappointment, vulnerability, resilience, compassion, and friendship. What part does fear play in each of your examples? What are you most afraid of? How do you manage your fears?

13. What is Jasper's role in the story? Describe his relationship with the other characters. Does Jasper remind you of someone you know or would like to know? Explain your answer.

14. Sarah narrates, "I hated that my brother's stupid haint story had gotten inside my head. I didn't believe in stuff like this. I believed in atoms and molecules. Not ghosts and curses." What does Sarah's fascination with the cosmos reveal about her? At what point is she able to put aside her need for scientific explanations? What changes her perceptions and her belief in the supernatural world? Have you ever believed in something as strongly as Sarah?

15. Which character do you relate to most? What makes you identify or connect with them? Which character is most unlike you? Who do you most admire in this story? Explain your answers.

16. Consider Sarah's and Jovita's friendship. How do the Jones Girls impact this friendship? Are you surprised by any of the girls' actions? What would you have done if you had been in Sarah's place? Sarah narrates, "Mama always told me forgiveness was not for the other person but for yourself." What do you think Sarah's mother meant by this?

17. What is the significance of the dead oak tree in the graveyard? What effect does it have on Sarah? What is the significance of Sophie's diary? What effects does it have on Mrs. Greene and Abner?

18. The author explores instances of historical racism, hatred, violence, prejudice, discrimination, and white supremacy. She also examines bias, intolerance, and other tensions that haunt present-day life in Warrenville and Alton. How do those historical themes relate to current-day issues? How do bias and prejudices affect characters' relationships? Consider Janie's personal bias against Sarah's academic curiosity and her views on small country towns. Consider negative judgements toward Mrs. Whitney. Cite other examples from the story and explain your findings.

19. How might a community begin to address some of the issues discussed in the above question? Think about characters' actions at the beginning and end of the story, and how their perspectives evolved. How might someone work to grow and better understand their surroundings?

20. Mrs. Greene is highly critical and full of bitterness. She insists on strict discipline and supervision for her grandchildren. What was your response to reading about such treatment? How did you feel after realizing the type of grief Mrs. Greene was carrying? Did it affect the way you viewed Mrs. Greene and her choices?

21. The Creek Church scenes are filled with imagery that conjures up intense feelings in Sarah's group. Describe your favorite details from these scenes. What did they add to your understanding of what was happening there?

22. Sarah narrates, "The Creek Church boy stood in a sliver of porch light without casting a shadow . . . I squinted as his mouth moved. He was trying to say something, but I couldn't understand him—I was too afraid to focus on anything." What do you think Abner was trying to say to Sarah? What do you think Sarah might have said to him if she hadn't been so afraid? If you could have spoken to him, what might you have said?

23. It's no secret that there are restless spirits haunting Warrenville. What do these spirits represent to the townspeople? Why had so many of them refused to address the issue and free their blood kin's spirits? What does it take to set things right and heal the town?

24. What parts of the story most held your interest? For what reasons? What scenes were the most suspenseful, surprising, disturbing, confusing, fascinating, heartwarming, inspiring, or humorous? Explain your answers.

25. In your opinion, what was Sarah's greatest moment? What was Janie's or Jasper's? Do you think Ellis had a greatest moment? How were these moments important to the story? Explain your answers.

26. Sarah's group faced multiple fears, sensing a purpose much greater than themselves. Have you ever had to confront your fears to do something you thought you lacked the courage to do? What was the result? What advice would you have for others in similar situations? Explain your answers.

27. What do you think is at the heart of this story? Has the novel changed your perspective about anything? What have you learned about yourself? Do you think you might do things differently in the future as a result of reading this book? Explain your answers.

Extension Activities and Further Reading

1. Choose a moment from the story and create a sense response to that scene. Think about your immediate thoughts, feelings, and emotions after reading the passage. Does any imagery come to mind? In your response, reflect on your visceral sense of experience; don't worry about remaining completely accurate to the text. Your response could be in the form of a painting, a collage, musical playlist, or any other form of expression that is meaningful to you.

2. Jasper says, "'Mrs. Whitney says we can't change the past, but we need to remember it. We need to acknowledge it and not hide it.'" The idea of bearing witness is important to all victims of prejudice and injustice. By bearing witness, others can stand up for those who aren't able to tell their own stories, empowering movements to fight against injustices.

Sometimes, to bear witness means using our own personal or cultural stories to speak out against wrongdoing. Write a poem, essay, short play, song, or choreograph a dance to tell your family's or your community's story. Pick an impactful experience to begin and explain how that has affected other moments or people. How might you express yourself with the hope of encouraging others to make the world a better place? Is there an experience you might want others to replicate, or something you've gone through that you'd like them to learn from and improve upon for the future?

3. Read *Astrophysics for Young People in a Hurry* by Neil deGrasse Tyson and Gregory Mone (2019). This guide to the cosmos invites readers to explore the mysteries of the universe and includes infographics, principles of scientific inquiry, and forty full-color illustrations. How do you think Sarah would have felt reading this book? What about Janie? What parts most excite you, and what would you like to learn more about?

4. Watch episodes of *Cosmos: A Spacetime Odyssey*, an Emmy and Peabody Award winner for educational content; this documentary television series explores the wonders of outer space with host and astro-physicist Neil deGrasse Tyson. Does it change your perspective on the world around you?

5. Read *Leon's Story* by Leon Walter Tillage, with collages created by Susan Walter Tillage. Leon Tillage was the son of a sharecropper growing up in rural North Carolina in the 1940s (2000). As a young boy, Leon remembers hiding in terror from the Klansmen as they made their night raids. This autobiography is based on a speech he gave at a school in Baltimore, Maryland, where he worked as a custodian. He wanted to bear witness to, as he says, "the uselessness of hatred and the senselessness of racism."

6. Read *A Wreath for Emmett Till* by Newbery Honor-winning author and poet Marilyn Nelson, and illustrated by Philippe Lardy. By honoring a young fourteen-year-old African American boy brutally murdered in Mississippi in 1955, Nelson draws attention to the story that helped fuel the civil rights movement of the late 1950s and 1960s. Nelson uses an intricate form of poetry that she refers to as a heroic crown of Italian sonnets, in which she encourages readers to speak out against violence and brutality and all

modern-day injustices. Think about poetry as a form of storytelling. How does it compare to reading a novel-length text? How does it capture emotions?

7. Consider reading other fiction and nonfiction with similar themes, settings, and characters:

Fiction

The Undefeated by Kwame Alexander, illustrated by Kadir Nelson

Ghost Boys by Jewell Parker Rhodes

Stella by Starlight by Sharon M. Draper

Midnight without a Moon by Linda Williams Jackson

This Is the Rope: A Story from the Great Migration by Jacqueline Woodson, illustrated by James Ransome

Witness by Karen Hesse

Freedom Over Me: Eleven Slaves, Their Lives and Dreams Brought to Life by Ashley Bryan

Nonfiction

Getting Away with Murder: The True Story of the Emmett Till Case by Chris Crowe

They Called Themselves the K.K.K: The Birth of an American Terrorist Group by Susan Campbell Bartoletti

This guide was written in 2019
by Judith Clifton, M.Ed, MS, Educational and Youth
Literary Consultant, Chatham, MA.

This guide has been provided by Simon & Schuster for classroom, library, and reading group use. It may be reproduced in its entirety or excerpted for these purposes.

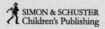